FIELD OF LOST SHOES
Official Novelization of the Feature Film

by

DAVID KENNEDY

With LOUISE PARSLEY *&* JOHN RIXEY MOORE

Copyright © 2014 by David Kennedy
All rights reserved.

Published in the United States by Field of Lost Shoes, LLC.

Except as permitted under the U.S. Copyright Act of 1976, no part of this book may be reproduced, scanned, or distributed in any printed or electronic form without written permission from the publisher. Please do not participate in or encourage piracy of copyrighted materials in violation of the author's rights.

Cover & interior design and editorial services provided by Kristina Blank Makansi, Treehouse Author Services, LLC
Cover images: Field of Lost Shoes, LLC

ISBN: 978-0-692-29507-6

to the Boys

Author's Notes

What you have in front of you is a novelization of the movie *Field of Lost Shoes*, a feature film produced by Thomas F. Farrell II and myself, executive produced by Brandon K. Hogan, written by Thomas F. Farrell, II, myself, and Ron Bass, and directed by Sean McNamara.

This a different kind of novel. It came into being after the movie was made, and is based strictly on the final version of the feature film.

It is my fervent hope that this novel will contribute to your understanding of and appreciation for this important story, based on actual events in our nation's history.

First off, let's put credit where credit is due. Telling this story was my partner's idea. Tom never gave up on the idea. He inspired others to join in the effort, including myself. What we have produced is testimony to Tom Farrell's vision and persistence. Thanks, Tom!

Field of Lost Shoes was, and continues to be, a team effort. I have included the full credits at the end of the novel to recognize those individuals who worked so hard to make it happen. I hope you will take time to read all the names.

Our movie was shot on location in Virginia during June of 2013, on the grounds of the Virginia Military Institute, at the Governor's Mansion in Richmond, at the State Capitol, at the Westover

Plantation on the James River, and at state property in Goochland County. It could not have been made without the active support of the Commonwealth of Virginia and the Virginia Film Office.

Readers are encouraged to link directly to photos on our fieldoflostshoesnovel.com website, where you will find screenshots taken from the movie itself that correspond to chapters in this novel.

Readers are also encouraged to listen to the stunning and emotional soundtrack for the movie by our Composer, Frederik Wiedmann, available on the La-La Land label.

Thanks to VMI for trusting us to tell their story.

Thanks to our investors, who made it all possible.

Thanks to my fellow authors, Louise Bayless Parsley and John Rixey Moore.

Thank you, the reader, for joining us on this journey.

This entire effort is dedicated, as Tom is known to remind us, "to the Boys."

— *David Kennedy*

FIELD OF LOST SHOES
Official Novelization of the Feature Film

Shenandoah

Come with me on a journey south. Fly with me on the wings of an eagle, high in the cool springtime air.

Climbing from the north, banking away from the sun-struck Potomac River, we turn southward over the Blue Ridge Mountains to discover the hidden green counterpane of an undulant fairyland, shouldered between ancient ridges now worn smooth by the slow violence of geology and mantled with old growth timber.

Shenandoah. Green and thriving. This is the fertile, isolated "Valley of Virginia." It is mid-May, and the fields are already in full bloom. On the sloping grasses, cattle dot the quiet hillsides and graze among swales of purple shadow. Wild deer stand at the edge of their forests like dancers, poised and alert, testing the air for information, while faded wooden barns, hand-built generations ago of rough-sawn planks, still perch precariously on their fieldstone foundations, keeping watch over impossibly steep knolls where the dark earth is whorled into a drapery of soft furrows. It is a feminine land, curving and languorous. Alluring and expectant. Beneath the stillness, Shenandoah is busy living, shaking off the gray of winter.

Descending along the western foothills of the Blue Ridge, the Allegheny Mountains rise sharply off to our right, These two mountain ranges, running in general parallel, carved here thousands of years ago by the retreating ice, have served to protect the Shenandoah for centuries. Since before colonial times, before the first white settlers, they have kept strangers out, sometimes discouraging even those who sought its bounty as a way of life, and sometimes entire armies that have tried to march into these hills with less wholesome intent.

Ahead, an abrupt ridge suddenly appears in the space between the mountains like the spine of some primordial sea beast breeching in the valley floor. This is Massanutten. To the locals this is a mountain, though small compared to the high ridges to the east and west. Running north and south for some twenty miles, this mass divides the valley, and settlers a few centuries ago who made a choice at random of which side to explore might have settled and lived out their lives without ever seeing those who chose the other.

At the southern end of Massanutten, where the spine dives back underground, the great valley continues. Today, the railroad town of Staunton, once a frontier settlement, is here, and farther to the south, across achingly beautiful cultivation, is the town of Lexington, Virginia. Today Lexington is home to more than seven thousand inhabitants and two respected institutions of higher learning, the Virginia Military Institute, and Washington and Lee University.

Many of Lexington's original buildings still crowd the main street, and along the few side streets they seem to huddle together, perhaps to help steady one another, or perhaps to share the view of this strange new century. In fact, there is a plaque in the center of the town that shows the entire original plot of Lexington, and it takes only a short walk for the visitor to see that the difference between the modern town and the proto-village is mostly just a matter of yardage. One hundred and fifty years ago, there were only a thousand or so living here. Some things change. Others do not.

At one end of the city, an impressive fortress rises up from the top of a hill. This is the Virginia Military Institute. Looking down on the main castle, her golden yellow stones and arches catch the light. We fly over top and see that the main castle is actually an open barracks, home to the Corps of Cadets, with four levels built up around the interior grassy-green square, and eight walkways leading to the center guardhouse. Around the top and open to panoramic fields of fire, rise the parapets of a crenelated castle. The battlements are no longer necessary of course, but they stand for something that is.

Just outside the barracks, there is a row of buildings that are an important part of the school. Among them, there is a church with traditional stained-glass windows and an academic building with serious countenance next to the church. This is a sacred place on the grounds. In front of this building is a large, tragic bronze statue mounted upon a stone base. The figure is of a seated woman, her head resting heavily upon her hand. She is in a deep and perpetual sadness from which she will never recover. She is the universal Mother mourning her dead. Below the statue, in the ground upon which she gazes, are the graves of five young men, now long dead. The stones bear their names, their VMI ranks, and where they were born. The dates of their deaths, all save one, are the same. Small U.S. flags and flags of Virginia hang forlornly at each headstone.

The seated woman faces outward, toward the green parade grounds and out past the massive barracks building, the flagpoles and nineteenth century field cannon, and across the main road which leads to the school grounds. Yet in her endless grief she is separate from the life and times that surround her. Her eyes are forever cast down.

Today, cadets are preparing for a parade. Two younger cadets help a cadet officer with his ceremonial dress uniform. They stretch a crimson band taunt around the officer's waist. They adjust belts and hand-polished ceremonial fittings. They know everything must be exactly right.

Company by company, the Corps of Cadets emerges from the

barracks and through the central archway facing the parade ground. Formal gray uniform coats with brilliant rows of brass buttons. Snow white trousers and shiny black boots. Arching, plumed hats held on with chin straps clasped in the mouth. Rifles at the shoulder, bayonets fixed. Cadet officers lead the way, swords drawn and carried against the shoulder. A red swallow-tail pennant leads of each company, as they march onto the parade ground to find their places in the larger formation. Smaller squares join larger ones as the Corps assembles on the sweeping parade field.

It is May 15, the day set aside every year to honor those over whom the statue stands watch, and, like so many years before, the main road is lined with family and friends as the long gray line of cadets, the color guard leading the way, marches forward followed by a band with drums and fifes and bagpipes. In front of the statue, in front of the woman who mourns, the current Commandant of Cadets and the Superintendent of the Institute stand in dress military uniform and salute on behalf of those who rest nearby.

Every year, a parade is held at VMI to honor cadets who gave their lives at a turning point during the American Civil War.

An honor guard of seven cadets takes its place behind the graves. On command, they raise their rifles and point them high into the air. The leader gives the command, and the sudden crack of gunfire rings out. The honor guard fires two more times in unison.

On May 15, 1864, seven friends marched into the Battle of New Market. Only four came out.

The Civil War and the battle in which those young patriots honored today lost their lives are the backdrops of our story. Young men forge friendships along different paths. Our story is that of seven friends—friends who laughed together, marched together, fought together—who embraced what they should be and, facing challenges well beyond their years, came to know what they could be. What they would be. But who were these boys? What of their families? Their hopes, their dreams? Were they cut from similar cloth or did they wear badges of differing backgrounds? If our sons and daughters today were in their shoes, could they compare ... or identify?

Any journey to an unfamiliar place or time can benefit from having a guide. Someone to get set the stage, orient us to our surroundings, and get us headed in the right direction. Our guide is a young man named John Wise.

To my comrades in arms, and to my fellow Virginians:

Virginians! You who in our day were led by Lee and Jackson! One who loves you wrote this story; one who was your comrade in the fight we lost; one who has no word of blame for you, but, on the contrary, believes that we had every provocation to fight; one who, as long as he lives, will glory in the way we fought, and is proud of his own scars, and teaches his children to believe that the record of Confederate valor is a priceless heritage.

It is not written when the truth can do you harm. It is not written by an alien in feeling, or an enthusiast for an abstract idea. It is written to make you think, to make you ask yourselves whether you can, before God, claim that all was as it should be when we had slavery. It is written to reconcile you to your loss by showing you from what your children were delivered.

It is penned in the firm belief that some day, while brooding upon the happiness, the wealth, the culture, the refinement then possessed by the South, and to so large an extent lost to her now, you may realize that all these, delightful as they were, did not justify the curse and misery of human slavery.

I seek to make you realize, if not admit, that its abolition was a greater blessing to us even than to the slaves, and that emancipation was worth all we surrendered, and all the precious lives that were destroyed; to bring you to confess, the brave and generous men I know you to be, that the time has come at last when, through our tears, and without disloyalty to the dead, in the possession of freedom and union and liberty, true Confederates, viewing it all in the clearer light and calmer atmosphere of today, ought to thank God that slavery died at Appomattox.

John S. Wise
September 10, 1899

1858

Governor's Mansion
Richmond, Virginia

The stately white columns of the grand home are bathed in the warm glow of lamplight as a formal carriage drawn by two horses pulls ups to the entrance. The evening air outside is cool, but inside young John Wise is reading stretched out by the fire.

> *When I was twelve years old, my father was governor of Virginia.*

John's father, Henry Alexander Wise, slowly descends the staircase, passing ornately framed paintings on the wall. He was elected to office in 1855 and is an impressive, well-dressed man. He reaches the ground floor, stops before a grandfather clock, pulls out his pocket watch, and checks it against the time on the clock.

> *None of us knew at that time, but our world was about to explode over the issue of slavery in America.*

The governor turns and looks toward a formal sitting room. His lips curve up in a smile at the sight of his son sprawled out on an ornate carpet in front of the fireplace.

My father's heart had long since changed on the topic.

Surrounded by a pile of books, John has his nose buried in one particular volume. He is dressed in a white shirt, vest, and bow tie, and his face is round and full.

*And one night, he took me to a place
that would forever change my own.*

Relishing the sight, the young man's father pauses, then interrupts.

"Reading the Englishman again?"

"Will I be shot for treason, father?" John asks, looking up with a smile.

"Most likely," the governor says with a laugh. "Another of those long titles, is it?"

"*The Personal History, Adventures, Experience and Observation of David Copperfield the Younger of Blunderstone Rookery—*" John proudly recites from memory before his father interrupts, finishing for him.

"—*Which He Never Meant to Publish on Any Account.*" The governor sits in a high back chair as John, clearly impressed, snaps the thick volume shut.

"You read it. I guess that's why it's here." John gets up and goes to his father.

"I suppose so," the governor says with a smile. "Get your coat, John. We're going to take a little ride."

The governor, cane in hand, and his son climb into the rear seat of the official carriage. They sit facing forward, next to one another, and John's long coat and soft brimmed cap ripple in the breeze as they ride through the streets of Richmond. John stares out as they roll past the fine townhomes and churches of the city, a pensive look on his face.

"I don't think I like these surprise trips anymore, father."

Beneath his top hat, the governor raises a knowing eyebrow. "Because they're usually lessons in life?"

"Exactly."

The carriage crosses a long, dimly lit bridge over a wide river, toward more lights in the distance.

"Well, tell me about the play your mother took you to in Philadelphia."

John pauses before answering, hesitant to start this particular discussion with his father. "You mean *Uncle Tom's Cabin*?"

"And why have we not talked about it?"

John turns away, gazes outside the carriage. "Because we'll disagree. And disagreeing with you is so … disagreeable."

With a knowing smile, the governor nods. Then persists. "Your mother said you were not impressed by it."

"I think it's all made up. By the people who don't like us."

The older man's face now grows serious, with a touch of sadness ,as he shifts his gaze forward. "Yes. Well. There's lots of those in Philadelphia."

Outside, the scenery gives way to fewer residences, some deserted buildings, stables. The carriage finally arrives at a plain, red-brick warehouse facing a shipping dock on the waterfront. A ship's horn blares out. As the carriage slows, a white man in a coat directs a line of black men in shirtsleeves forward.

The carriage pulls to a stop in front of a sloping ramp leading up to the warehouse entrance. Over the top end of the building is a sign reading "Lumpkin's Jail" and another announcing "Auction House." A red flag is displayed from one of the brick arches and flaming torches light the exterior.

Through open brick archways, the glow of lights reflects the movements of a crowd already inside and busy. In the background, the voice of an auctioneer calls out, "All right, ladies and gentlemen. We're about to get started. Step on up, step on up. You're gonna love what we have in store tonight."

The carriage door swings open. Young John climbs out onto the dirt and takes a step forward. He looks up at the rough building, takes in the signs and the flags. "A slave auction?"

The governor steps down, but remains at the open carriage door as he, too, looks up at the façade. "Doubtless, those people in Philadelphia would not approve."

John, long coat and hat in place, starts up the ramp. At the top he turns, realizing his father has no intention of joining him. "You're not coming?"

Remaining standing behind the carriage door, the governor smiles. "John, I've never known you to need help making up your own mind."

The governor takes another weary, sad, and lingering look up at the building and turns to leave young John alone to experience first-hand what goes on inside Lumpkin's Jail. On his own, John turns back and continues up the ramp, removing his hat and heading through one of the brick archways, curious to see what is happening on the other side. A voice booms out, "O-yea, o-yea! Step on up, ladies and gentleman, the sale is about to begin."

Lumpkin's Jail

Inside the air is thick with sweat and pungent cigar smoke, and the room is dark and squalid, lit by smoking, flickering lamps. A group of buyers, mostly men but with a sprinkling of women, eye the merchandise, eager for the sale to begin. John hangs at the rear, electing to observe from the back of the room and glad no one recognizes him as the governor's son.

On a raised front stage, a hawker in top hat and mismatched clothing acts as master of ceremony and auctioneer. "A fine lot of slaves, belonging to the estate of the late Colonel William Jasper of

Amelia, sold for no fault but to settle the estate," he calls out, rousing the crowd. "We got all kinds: old ones, young ones, men and women, gals and boys."

On either side of the stage, slaves are positioned by handlers to move to the center when called. One prospective bidder checks out one of the male slaves in line, brutishly opening the man's jaw to check his mouth and teeth as other bidders inspect his eyes, arms, and legs, manhandling them as one would a horse. The hawker continues, "and as you may or may not know, Colonel Jasper's plantation slaves made him a pretty penny for the last twenty years."

Taking it all in, John studies the white men as they consider the merchandise, yet his gaze drifts back to and lingers on the slaves.

In the crowd, a black woman tends to the crowd of customers, handing out drinks on a platter, edging between and around the seated bidders. The hawker enthusiastically builds excitement for the upcoming bidding, joking.

"Gentlemen, what we have to offer here is so damn good, ol' Mr. Lumpkin even up and married one of 'em!" Derisive laughter fills the room and attention turns to the black woman carrying the platter of drinks. For a moment, we see anger flash in the eyes of Mary Lumpkin as she looks back up at the hawker.

At the edges of the open room, buyers continue to check out and inspect the offerings. "You won't find a mark of a whip an a one of 'em. We're not talking some low-class, Louisiana branding-iron stock!" John's gaze is diverted to a young slave girl, about his age, standing in a group further back from the stage, in line and awaiting her turn. Their eyes meet, and despite the surroundings and her situation, the pretty girl manages a gentle smile. They're around the same age, and yet their circumstances are so different.

The hawker continues. "We got the best slave stock from all of Central Virginia here tonight. Colonel Jasper's staff represents the finest stock in the state."

Locking eyes with the young girl, John exchanges a shy smile as he slowly scans the silhouette of her printed dress. Just below the notch of her bosom, the young girl's stomach takes a smooth but pronounced arc outward—she is very pregnant.

The hawker leans down at the edge of the stage to where different group of slaves are gathered, facing the crowd. "This is the best group of dining room servants, farmhands, cooks, milkers, seamstresses, washerwomen..." He puts his hand under the chin of a frightened young slave girl as he lands his point "...and a most promising group of sassy young females just ready to breed." The heavy night air is scratched by the buyers' abrasive laughter. One accentuates the point by smiling and popping the thick ash off his cigar.

Away from the stage, the young girl whose eyes met with John's realizes that John sees she is pregnant. Her smile gives way to embarrassment. She looks down and gently moves her open hand to rest on top of the baby inside. John is also embarrassed, and saddened. He tries to keep his friendly smile, but looks back to the stage and swallows, awkwardly.

The hawker finally gets the bidding started. He leads out a healthy woman slave in her mid to late twenties and walks her toward a slightly raised stand at the left of the stage. "Martha Ann, here, is the favorite of the household. Perfectly healthy, no blemish at all." He spins her around for all to see. Then he puts his hand under her chin to proudly display Martha Ann's frightened face, adding, "Look at that complexion."

He motions for the rest of the family to be brought out and placed to the right side of the stage. A white handler brings out her husband, Israel, who clutches two young children, a little boy about five and a girl about eight, in front of him. The children are confused and frightened. They keep their heads bowed, their gazes toward the floor. The hawker starts his sales pitch. "I offer Martha Ann at a reduced price, because it is the wish of all concerned to keep them together." He points to Israel, a slave in his early thirties. "Now Israel here is not what you'd call an 'able-bodied' man having broke his leg in the field which didn't exactly mend right. But he can do all kinds of light work, and you can have him and the young'uns mighty cheap." Israel boldly sees his chance and makes a desperate plea, "Masters, if you'll buy me, the children, and Martha Ann, God knows I'll work myself to death."

His wife, Martha Ann, still separated on the other side of the stage, looks on her husband, her face flushed with hope and pride while the faces of the potential buyers remain apathetic, unmoved by Israel's plea.

The hawker kicks off the bidding. "We'll start the bidding at four hundred." The room is silent. No motion at all. "Do I hear four hundred?"

Suddenly, an older man in a straw hat jabs up four fingers to his throat to bid.

"All right, we have four hundred, do I hear four fifty?" The hawker is clearly frustrated. "Come on people, four fifty. Look at her. He can work." The children squirm. Israel nervously holds the boy and girl close together. Martha Ann's eyes plead out to the crowd for deliverance.

John grows more and more uncomfortable as he watches the sale unfold. He swallows hard and looks around.

The hawker jabs at the buyers. "This is one of the best slave lots we're gonna see all night, gentlemen." The hawker gives up. "Four hundred going once, four hundred going twice…." The buyers' faces show no emotion. "Sold."

He points to the winning bidder and asks, "Will you take Israel and the young'uns with her?"

Martha Ann holds her breath. John waits.

"No." The old man stands and makes his way to the stage to claim his purchase. "I'm lucky to be able to afford one as it is."

Martha Ann screams out in disbelief and agony, thrusts her arms out to the crowd, pleading. The old man continues as he waddles through the crowd to the front, impatient to be done with this. "I don't need no more mouths to feed than hers."

Martha begs in desperation. "No! Please!" Tears stream down her face as she moves toward Israel and her children, only to be blocked and pulled back by one of the handlers.

The children shriek out and rush for their mother. They are at first held back, but the little ones finally wriggle free and reach her. Israel reaches the center of the stage where the family clutches one other in desperation as more of the hawker's assistants join in to break them up and to restore order.

The crowd observes placidly as the family is pulled apart, and Israel and the children are dragged to the right while Martha Ann is pulled away to the left, screaming and pleading for her family.

John cannot look away, and the brutal event seems to unfold slowly, prolonging the agony as the family continues to shriek and cry out for one another.

The old man has Martha Ann by the hand, tearing her from her children as he roughly leads her away, down from the stage, and through the crowd. He cynically reassures her, "You'll have more children, missy, you'll see." Shrieking, Martha Ann reaches back and makes one final gesture to her family. Then, as quickly as it happened, the disruption is cleared and the hawker is set to resume his chant while the crowd, unmoved by the family's separation, is likewise ready to resume bidding on the next lot.

John, his eyes wide in disbelief, is unable to endure another minute of the auction. He turns away, steps back through the brick awning and onto the walkway surrounding the outside of the warehouse. He crushes his hat in his hand and walks quickly along the platform to escape. His walk turns into a trot and then into a run as tears of anger and disbelief stream down his cheeks.

Five Years Later

Virginia Military Institute

The tears tracking down twelve-year-old John Wise's face from that night at the slave auction are long gone, and the privileged, young boy running from Lumpkin's Jail has grown into an intense young man. John is still running, only now he's wearing a uniform and carrying a heavy Austrian musket. Now a cadet at the Virginia Military Institute, John has grown into a handsome young man with chiseled features and focused, intense eyes looking out from beneath his arched military cap with the brass insignia of a castle and an eagle across the front, topped by a black-feathered plume. In his gray wool military uniform jacket—complete with three rows of shiny brass buttons and a high collar in front—white trousers, and black boots, he runs with a steady, relentless, military pace across the broad green parade ground that arches out in front of the main, castle-like building of his school. In front of the building, a statue of George Washington stands on a high pedestal, flanked by a row of wagon-wheeled cannon below. John heads for the arched entrance to the castle.

Five years later, the Civil War began closing in on the Shenandoah Valley, a place that was the home of the military school to which my father had sent me when he became a general in the Confederate Army.

I was seventeen years old and in my second year at the Virginia Military Institute.

Inside the VMI castle, a huge quadrangle is surrounded by four rising floors of rooms whose doors and windows open to guard-railed walkways overlooking the central quad. A civilian college would call this a dormitory. For the cadets of VMI, this is a barracks. And it is their home. Eight separate dirt paths from the corners and centers of each side of the quadrangle converge at a center guard shack. We have been here before. We have seen the cadets form up and march in honor of their fallen brethren. But now, it is more than one hundred fifty years earlier, and the young cadets of the Virginia Military Academy have not yet been called to arms.

Matriculation Day for Young "Sir Rat"

Matriculation - to be added to a list;
from Latin matricula (little list)

A mix of cadets in uniform and new students in civilian clothing mill about the quadrangle. One new student pushes a cart with a heavy box on it. Another drags a heavy chest along the path. Some cadets sit on chairs. Others stand in circles, talking.

One young arrival tries to stop a uniformed cadet for directions, but the cadet barely notices him and hurries by. The young arrival looks about for help and then gives up. He couldn't be more than thirteen or fourteen, with the look of an adorable boy whose Mommy dressed him in his best Sunday clothes—right down to the oversized and wilting bow tie, suit coat, and floppy, billed hat that can barely contain his sweeping curls of long brown hair. Only a mother's heart would go out to him as he sits on his heavy, bulky clothing chest, pulls out a paper, from his vest pocket and unfolds it. Reads. Looks around for clues. Shakes his head.

From a second-floor overlook, two upper class cadets, Sam Atwill and Duck Colonna, share a laugh as they look down at the quad in detached amusement, watching the new students wander about lost and confused, out of place in their civilian clothes. Dark-haired, barrel-chested Duck looks sharp and quite the military soldier in a clean dress uniform, brass-buttoned coatee, and white pants, with a formal plumed cap on his head. Impressive gold rank stripes decorate the arms of his uniform. Blond-haired Sam, in contrast, is hatless. His hair is wild and out of place. His gray uniform coatee is unbuttoned and relaxed, and Sam definitely doesn't have any corporal, sergeant, or any other rank insignia attached. But Sam's smile does light up the conversation. Duck perks up at something he notices below. He slaps Sam on the shoulder and points, and both cadets shake their heads and smile.

It's John Wise, running through the quad, musket still in hand, edging carefully around the confused new arrivals.

Sam leans forward onto the guardrail, cups his hands to his mouth, and shouts out, "Whoa! Johnny Wise! Always in a hurry!"

Below, John doesn't hear the call. He's intent on getting where he's going, and so he makes his way through the quad and exits our view. Duck and Sam shift attention back to the quad below them. The poor, adorable boy in the floppy hat has his paper out again, asking for directions. Again, he is ignored. Duck gets an idea, brightens up, and elbows Sam as he points down at the lost child.

"Think he'll do?" He quickly answers his own question. "He's a rabbit, a mouse."

Sam's eyes light up in agreement. "He's perfect. It's like he's shipped in from heaven. Round up the boys!"

Sam slaps Duck on the arm and heads out. Duck smiles in agreement, nods. "All right."

Below, the boy bites his lip in frustration. He stands up, looks around, shakes his head again, then folds his instruction paper back up and tucks it in a pocket.

Sam has an eye on his prey. He pulls on an informal, comfortable military billed cap to complete his uniform and walks briskly across the quad, slapping acquaintances on the shoulder without disrupting his concentration.

The new kid doesn't see Sam approaching. Before he knows it, Sam takes hold of the youngster's trunk by the side handles and lifts it up.

"Good morning, young sir! Let me give you a hand to the barracks!"

The kid stares, star-struck and confused.

"But sir, you are an upperclassman."

Sam has the awkward chest in hand and isn't slowing down. He looks back over his shoulder at the youngster, and they head for the stairs.

"This is true, but one day, you'll be magnificent yourself and somehow find a way to repay my kindness." Sam keeps heading for the stairs, chest swinging in front. The kid is dazzled at this bit of good luck. Relieved, he busts out with a huge smile and rushes to keep up.

The Barracks

Inside a simple VMI barracks room, a cadet sits, hat on his head and feet on the central, shared desk, methodically wiping down a musket. Another cadet, dark-haired and with a furrowed look of concentration on his face, also sits at the desk, intently scratching at a paper with a piece of drawing charcoal in his fingers. Other muskets are lined in a rack, bedrolls are stacked in a corner, and shelves with formal headgear on the top rows, books on the bottom rows make the room as homey as a barracks can be. Duck, who has returned from his errand, is already back and putting his hat on the shelf behind the desk when the door bangs open and Sam and the youngster enter the room, Sam waddling in first with the heavy trunk.

"Well, imagine this, a welcoming committee! Robert, come in and meet some of the boys. This here is Duck."

Duck steps up with a knowing grin and takes the chest from Sam. "Let's get you unpacked."

Young Robert starts to object, but it's too late, and the older cadets are clearly in control as Sam begins introducing the other boys. He starts off by pointing to the cadet with his feet up on the desk, musket in hand. "Now this is Jack Stanard. A real soldier and a hard man, indeed. If you want to grow up to be a man, you pay attention to him and not to me."

Stanard scowls, and his hard look and stern eyes show he is not one to joke around. "If you're looking for an easy ride, you've come to the wrong place."

Duck digs into the youngster's trunk as Sam curls around the desk and puts his arm around the cadet who is intent on sketching on a piece of paper with charcoal. Sam interrupts, explaining to the young arrival, "This handsome creature is our resident Jew. His name is actually Moses, and he's an artist." Moses looks up shyly, gives a friendly wave. Moses Ezekiel is slender, tall, and darkly handsome. There is kindness in his eyes. Sam continues, "He's got the best heart of the bunch, so if you ever need to cry on somebody's shoulder...."

Moses interrupts gently, "We'll start with my telling you all about Sammy here. So you can protect yourself." Sam laughs and peeks over Moses' shoulder. Sam's eyebrows lift. Moses tilts the paper away, hiding it, but Sam playfully snatches it away. Moses gives up, lets Sam have it. It's a charcoal sketch of a pretty young girl, and Sam admires it with a glint in his eyes.

"Could you do another one of them ... but without the clothes?" Moses smiles but reaches to retrieve his drawing as Sam laughs his mischievous laugh.

An interruption from Duck jolts the mood. "Uh-oh. What

have we here?" All eyes turn to Duck. Frowning, his face stern, he pulls a string of sausages from Robert's chest and holds them up for everyone to see.

The youngster is confused. "What … what is that?"

All eyes focus on the youngster. Sam jumps in, a bit stunned. "That looks like food to me, son. Anyone tell you there's a war going on?" Sam's tone darkens. "Concealed foodstuffs, that's contraband."

Duck quickly adds. "Clear violation of Institute regulations. Immediate dismissal."

"Might even be criminal," adds Sam. Young Robert still stands near the doorway, confused. Sam approaches him. "Oh, Bobby, how could you?"

The new arrival is clearly flustered and at a loss for words. He struggles to answer, but Sam motions for the youngster to be silent and considers what must be done. He looks to Stanard and speaks quietly. "Cadet Stanard, could you please fetch the Officer of the Day?"

Perturbed, Stanard rises slowly, musket still in hand, and ambles out, brushing the youngster's shoulder back as he goes by. Moses, still seated at the desk with his drawings, watches in silence, knowing what is in store.

Agonized and unsettled, Young Robert sputters in protest. "I … I don't know how it got there."

Standing in judgment, Sam raises his hand to silence the boy.

Stanard soon returns to the room, leading the way, with another Cadet, Garland Jefferson, seventeen, blond, tall, and thin, close behind him. Jefferson carries himself with an aristocratic bearing and is dressed in formal uniform, with a soft-billed cap on his head.

Jefferson crosses his arms in front of his chest. His cold gray eyes pierce poor Robert, who looks up, trembling. Sam breaks the silence and addresses Robert, "This is Cadet Garland Jefferson, Officer of the Day, whose jurisdiction covers this matter." The youngster can barely look up at the towering, menacing figure. "And since his family are direct descendants of Thomas Jefferson and own the eighth largest plantation in—"

"That'll do, Atwill." Jeffersons's deadpan cuts Sam short.

All in the room fall deathly silent. Robert takes short breaths, terrified and trembling.

"Now, if I take charge," Jefferson says in a slow drawl, "this goes to the faculty. It ends horribly for the boy." Robert sinks further into confusion and despair. He pleads. "Oh, please, Sir...."

Sam looks up to the towering Jefferson. "Could we have Duck fetch John Wise? Handle this within the barracks?" Jefferson studies Sam, considers the request. Then he nods once, in approval. Sam flashes a look to Duck, who reaches back to the shelf, grabs his formal headgear, then heads past the desk and out the door, the nails in the soles of his formal shoes clomping by on the wooden floor.

Stanard goes back to wiping down his musket, and Garland Jefferson walks around the desk to look over Moses's shoulder to observe his drawing. Robert stands in silence, trying not to dissolve into tears of agony.

After a tortuous moment, Duck returns with John Wise. John is meticulously attired, and he holds his cap crisply under his left arm. He enters the room and stops. Sam arcs behind the youngster, puts a hand on his shoulder, and spins Robert to face John Wise. "Bobby, this is John Wise. Our unofficial Chief Magistrate." John towers above Bobby. He looks down at the frightened youngster as Sam continues. "Now, his father was once the governor of this commonwealth, so he is as close to an aristocrat as you can find in a democracy."

Sam gives Robert another nudge forward. John bends down to be eye to eye with the youngster. The young boy struggles to look up, fear flashing in his eyes along with welling tears. He can't hold John's gaze. "Look me in the eyes, son." Bobby looks away, then back to John. "Tell me the truth as if your very life depended on it." Robert takes a big gulp. John continues, "Did you do this?"

"Oh no, sir," Robert bursts out. "I swear on my father's soul." Just then, a huge single tear streams down the youngster's cheek.

John considers him carefully, then rises and addresses the room, confidently.

"I believe this child." John turns to Garland. "I ask that we be allowed to settle this here in the barracks." Garland considers, then nods and mutters, "All right."

John now turns back to the frightened youngster. "You understand, son, that if this gets out, it would be bad for Cadet Jefferson." He walks past Robert, past the desk, and puts his plumed hat in its position on the bookcase's shelf. He then slides something off the top of the shelf. "Therefore, there must be evidence of punishment. Will you submit to a caning?"

John takes what he slid off the top shelf and places it into the hands of Garland. It is a three-foot-long, sturdy-handled whip.

Tears roll out of Robert's eyes. With an uncanny mix of fear and grace, Robert says, "Oh yes, sir. And thank you for being so … merciful." With that, Garland snaps the cane against the desk, testing it out. The noise makes Robert wince and jump in place. Duck motions to Robert and smiles a wicked smile. "Take your shirt off." Terrified, Robert hurriedly unbuttons his coat. Garland cracks the cane against the desk again. Robert winces as the cane smacks wood.

Robert pulls off his coat, revealing a billowing white shirt and suspenders. He unbuttons and pulls off the shirt, exposing a young boy's pale, soft, undernourished torso. Duck and John both smile, but Moses is not amused. His face betrays concern, and he looks away.

Robert is now stripped to the waist. John puts a hand on his shoulder and pushes him forward to the front edge of the desk. His back is thin and pale. The other cadets clear the area and take positions around to watch the beating. Bobby faces the desk and, garnering all the strength and courage a young boy can gather, starts to lean forward into the position for caning.

John takes a chair, reverses it, and sits in front of Robert, who now turns around, shaking in fear, looking from side to side at those who surround him. Robert now looks lightly down toward John. John looks the youngster in the eye.

"First-year cadets are known as rats. You are a rat." Something in John's tone softens. "But you're a special rat, understand? You are my rat. And under my protection." He looks around. "And under the protection of all here." Robert's eyes are looking around the room. He is totally confused. Behind him, Sam and Duck share a knowing smile.

John continues, "Are you with us, Robert?"

The youngster is confused. "Oh, yes. Oh yes, sir."

Now even Stanard and Sam exchange a smile as John goes on. "I want you always to remember the horrible injustice you thought was going to befall you here today. Of one human being using his authority over another without decency or conscience." The cadets now draw closer in around Robert. "And of the need to instill a code of honor that transcends the temptations of power." Behind and unseen by Robert, Moses also smiles a smile of relief.

John Wise now stands up, moves the chair out of the way, and stands in front of Robert, towering above him. He takes the whip from Jefferson and holds it firmly in his right hand.

"I hereby raise you above the level of common rat." Robert looks confused, still not sure exactly what is taking place. His eyes are glued on the whip as John takes it, raises it up, then brings it down gently onto Robert's left shoulder, with a tap, then raises it over Robert's head to the other shoulder in the barracks' own knighting ceremony. "You shall be known in this company as … Sir Rat."

At that, all the cadets clap, and smiles ring the room. Even Jack Stanard manages a smirk. Garland Jefferson beams and gives the youngster a reassuring tug on the shoulder. Sam shoves a bundle of clothing into Robert's arms. "Now put your shirt on, son. Before we find ourselves a healthier specimen." Robert, now and henceforth known simply as "Sir Rat," smiles through tears of relief.

John changes the subject quickly. "You hungry, boy?"

Sir Rat smiles and answers, "Oh, yes, sir."

The mood lightens as John looks around at the room. "Well, what do you gentlemen say to a little 'midnight requisition'?"

All but Sir Rat smile and nod. Puzzled, he asks, "What?"

"Never mind." Sam smiles his mischievous smile again. "It's a tradition."

Old Judge

Nighttime. But for scattered lampposts and dimly lit lanterns, darkness covers the Institute.

Outside the main fortress sits a single-story red brick bakery boasting a brick oven and a sturdy wood table stacked with platters of freshly cooked loaves of bread. A blazing fire inside sends streams of warm light through the windows, checkering the ground outside.

In the shadows, figures slide by the side window, pause at the corner, then steal toward the front door. Out for an adventure, the boys are in good spirits, and in hushed whispers, they bump into one another in the dark, laughing and shushing each other.

"Ah, that does smell good," a cadet says.

John Wise drops to his knees. "Help me with this doorknob," he says as he works on the stubborn fixture. A moment passes, and he finally gets it unlatched. The door creaks. "Shhh!" He slowly turns the handle, then cracks the door open just enough for him and the rest of the cadets to wiggle through inside. The door closes behind them with a clunk.

At the table, they behold a feast for hungry eyes and empty stomachs. The cadets prowl softly, trying not to make too much noise, but the smell of freshly baked bread is too much.

"Can I have some?" says one.

"That one is mine," says another.

"Let's get us some bread, boys," Garland Jefferson announces as grandly as he can under his breath. Their feast is about to begin when the front door slams shut. Their heads snap around to see a massive black man blocking their only way out.

Anderson Dandrige, known to all as "Old Judge," the Institute's head cook and baker, holds a lamp in one hand, a menacing meat cleaver in the other. He drives the meat cleaver down into a nearby chopping block, sinking the steel edge deep into the wood. Panic radiates from Sir Rat's eyes.

Unafraid, John looks up and smiles. "Well, now." John respectfully greets the master of the bakery. "Evenin', Judge."

Sam notices Sir Rat shaking in fear. "No need to be afraid of Old Judge, boy," he tells the frightened youngster.

"He's just a grumpy old slave," Garland adds.

Old Judge moves stealthfully around the table toward Garland.

Now nose-to-nose with Garland, Old Judge sets the record straight. "I may be the property of the Institute," he begins, "but I have the ear of the superintendent and the full trust and confidence of the commandant." His eyes lock with Garland's as Old Judge hammers home, "I'm the master of this bakery!"

Moses Ezekiel, standing back next to the chopping block, quietly looks down at the menacing knife and observes in a low voice, "You also have a cleaver."

Old Judge looks over the cadets. His voice stern and filled with absolute authority, he reprimands them. "There's nothing worse in a time of conflict than a thief of food."

Sam continues to chew on a mouthful of warm bread, relishing each bite, yet filled with guilt, while John moves quickly and confidently around the table to where Old Judge stands, formidably holding his lamp up to Garland's face with Sir Rat huddled beside the older cadet. John puts his hand on young Sir Rat's shoulder, looks down, and prompts the youngster, "Tell him why we're here, son."

Sir Rat responds with the disarming innocence of a child. "We ... we're real hungry, Mr. Judge. And those loaves smell awful good."

Old Judge looks down on the youngster as Sir Rat continues, "I'm new here, but Mr. Wise here tells me the bread is the best part of this school."

At that, Old Judge's face softens. He looks down at the young boy, barely repressing a smile. The change in Old Judge's demeanor is not lost on Garland. Old Judge lets out, "Go ahead and get yourself one of those loaves, son. I suspect I can spare three or four."

Garland leans toward him, smiling. "Thank you, Judge." Moses, a serious look still on his face, humbly tips his cap in respect.

Relieved and grateful, the boys step forward, tearing off pieces of the steaming bread. Sir Rat puts a piece in his mouth, savors it, and leans his head back, enjoying the moment with unguarded ecstasy.

John moves around for a one-on-one with Old Judge. He and Old Judge move aside to speak in private, and with the boys busy eating in the background, negotiations begin.

"I'm not here for a handout, Judge," John says and then pauses, keeping a positive tone as he continues. "I'm here to negotiate a business arrangement." Old Judge cautiously studies the young man's face.

John continues, "You've seen the best of us on the shooting range."

Old Judge nods toward the boys and interjects, "Jewish boy is the best." He looks back to John and concedes, "Then you."

John quickly lays out the proposal. "We'll bring in some squirrel, rabbit, some possum. Harvest a fugitive chicken or two. Your people share in the meat. In return, we liberate some bread."

Old Judge considers. His face grows more serious. He likes the boys, John Wise especially, but it's a point of fact that they do not share the same legal or societal status. Narrowing his eyes, he gets to the crux of the matter.

"You see, the terms of this arrangement are a little more … serious … for some parties than for others."

Point taken.

John puts his hand on Old Judge's shoulder and counters with a solemn promise. "If this comes crashing down, it will not fall on you." There is an unspoken agreement. A pledge given, a pledge accepted. The two men are now co-conspirators and partners in righteous criminal activity as behind them the other cadets continue their feast.

From This Day Forward, the Game Changes

The White House. March 29, 1864

Approaching a side entrance of the White House, a single horse pulls a simple, open-sided carriage carrying two passengers. Two Union soldiers in blue uniforms stand guard over the entryway to the East Wing. Women in long, hooped dresses and men in top hats stroll by. The grounds are manicured, but sparse.

Inside, silhouetted in the light of a tall window, President Abraham Lincoln confers with Secretary of State William H. Seward. Seward, an older, balding and rotund, gentleman, is easily a head shorter than the tall, lanky president.

With a long face grooved with deep lines, emblematic of the responsibility of a commander in chief at war, the president appears exhausted. Not expecting good news, Lincoln probes his secretary of state for answers. "Tell me this one is different."

"We ... think so. He's not afraid to take action," Seward says, guardedly optimistic. "That's a welcome change from your other generals."

Lincoln nods, as if each movement constitutes its own war

against weariness.

Below their window, a Union general, bearded and rumpled as if weariness is his constant companion, looks out from his carriage. His blue wool uniform coat is unbuttoned, and he clutches his hat as the steps are lowered. He surveys his surroundings, then climbs from the carriage onto the gravel driveway. Three gold stars mark each shoulder epaulet.

Inside, Lincoln voices his concern. "Some call Grant a butcher."

"Well, sir, that may be precisely what we need."

Lincoln nods. Seward's response confirms what the president already knows yet is hesitant to admit. He turns and slowly walks away from the window and out of the formal oval dining room. Rounding the corner, Lincoln heads into an adjacent waiting room where Grant waits with two uniformed military aides.

While still walking, Lincoln warmly greets his guest. "General. Congratulations on your victory. And your promotion."

Standing a full head taller than the rumpled victor of Chattanooga, Lincoln looks down as he shakes the general's hand. He turns to the other men in the room and signals his intent to speak with Grant in private. "Gentlemen, thank you."

The aides, another general and a colonel, along with Seward, take their leave, and a servant closes the curtains behind them, leaving Lincoln and Grant alone. Lincoln sits first, then Grant takes the seat across from him.

"They say you are the general the nation has been praying for," the president says. Grant listens, stolid and expressionless. "They also say you fight like a savage."

With no sign of emotion, Grant quickly says, "I would agree with both." Lincoln studies the man in front of him, and after a pause, Grant continues. "War is not opera, not theater, it is for winning. Winning ends the death. Ends the destruction. Begins the healing."

"And to win, brutality is required?"

"Each game has its rules, Mr. President. Are we to play chess? Or war?"

Lincoln leans forward, and in a measured tone, the president challenges. "And if I were to name you General in Chief...?"

Grant responds without hesitation, punching his words. "I will attack our enemy at all places and at all times. I will take away his crops, his animals, the food he has sheltered, his railroads, his industry, his clothing, his ammunition, his gunpowder, his steel, his armament, his salt." Then, striking a painful nerve for the man he serves, Grant continues, "and I will take from him the flower of his youth." The general takes a deliberate side look to the photo of a young boy resting on the fireplace mantle. It is a print of Lincoln's son Willie, eleven years old when he died. Grant knows full well that the loss of Willie is the president's greatest family heartbreak.

Lincoln also looks at the photo, his pain palpable, and Grant looks back into Lincoln's eyes. "I will destroy everything my enemy loves, and anything that might give him the means or hope to prevail."

The look holds between them. Stalwart and unblinking. Grant leans forward to ask, "Do you see me as a monster, Mr. President?"

Lincoln pauses. With intent, he, too, leans forward and replies with confidence. "I see you as a true general."

The Wolf Will Come
Shenandoah Valley Overlooking the New Market Gap

Two Confederate soldiers, one much older than the other, ride up a verdant, grass-covered hill. A lake of brown water stretches out in the lowland background behind them, surrounded by lush, green fields hemmed by white fences.

At the crest of the hill, the men stop and look out at the valley beyond. Villages and towns rise on either side of a central roadway, and, in the distance, a distinctive gap slices through the mountain range, marking the point where one mountain tapers off and another rises up.

Confederate General John C. Breckinridge, former Vice President of the United States, points toward the horizon and says, "The only way back across the Blue Ridge and into our flank is way down there ... the New Market Gap." He nods to the distinctive dip between the distant green mountains. "And that's where Grant will send them."

Major Charles Semple is not so sure. He shifts forward in the saddle, betraying discomfort. "Well, sir, General Lee does not believe an attack will come this spring." Semple is a handsome officer and an educated gentleman who carries himself with confidence. Like many other Americans, Semple is a recent immigrant, and he speaks with an Irish accent.

Breckinridge's confidence is unshaken, and he shoots back, "Well, General Lee is dead wrong. The Federals will come. And soon."

Breckinridge is none too happy with the situation in which he finds himself. He's been charged with defending the valley by General Robert E. Lee, commanding general of the Confederate Army of Northern Virginia, but he disagrees with his superior officer on strategy and finds himself dangerously behind schedule and hopelessly under-resourced. He pauses, then adds, "And I am going to need everything they've got."

Obligated to recommend a note of caution, Semple says, "Sir, you're asking me to tell command that General Lee is wrong."

Breckinridge looks over at his aide and responds with defiant humor. "Well, thank God you've been listening. I won't have to repeat myself."

Semple chooses not to argue, instead looking back out over the valley

Breckinridge points again to the gap and says, "If General Grant is the wolf, and we are the lamb, then New Market Gap is surely our throat." After a long pause, he adds, "And trust me, the wolf will come."

Drilling the Battalion

The temperature rises relentlessly as the summer sun bakes the young men in their heavy gray wool uniforms. They shoulder them proudly, but their Austrian muskets are hot and heavy. Seven groups of cadets, standing eight across and four deep, form up in front of the opening arch and statue of George Washington on the parade ground in front of the barracks of Virginia Military Institute. The battalion is grouped by cadet companies, and Superintendent Colonel Francis H. Smith, known as "Old Spex" to the cadets, stands in front of the formation in his Confederate dress uniform.

"Shoulder, arms!" His voice is rough and in response, muskets smack in well-ordered unison. "Order, arms!" Muskets smack in unison again.

A crowd of spectators watches the impressive display of military precision from behind the fatherly superintendent. Faculty officers in their crisp uniforms, young children, and ladies in colorful dresses and hooped skirts, many holding parasols, look on as the old man issues orders and the young men move as one organic unit to execute them.

Faculty officer Captain Henry A. Wise, known to all the cadets as "Chinook" sits tall in the saddle as he rides between the front and rear groups keeping a careful eye on the young men.

In the shade of a nearby porch, young girls in flowing dresses and bonnets sip drinks in crystal sherry glasses as the sun beats down without mercy. More commands are issued, and more strenuous exercise follows.

"Order, arms!"

In one of the front groups, young Sir Rat struggles with his heavy rifle. His lower lip droops and his eyes sag as he waivers in the ranks.

"Order, arms!"

Sir Rat, now clearly in trouble, is about to pass out from heat exhaustion. To his right, Moses Ezekiel notices him wobble and looks on, concerned, while behind the boy, Sam Atwill watches. John Wise also keeps an eye on the youngster.

Succumbing momentarily to the heat, Sir Rat staggers backward, but Sam catches him and pushes him forward enough to hold him in position. Sir Rat catches himself and mumbles, "I'm okay."

Garland Jefferson, to Sam's left and also in the row behind Sir Rat, shares the others' concern as he sees Sir Rat tilt and sway. Meanwhile, the sun beats down as the superintendent continues the drill.

"Order, arms!" Sir Rat keeps up, but only with great exertion.

Duck Colonna, the cadet sergeant supervising the activity, paces alongside the left of the formation, sword in hand. His face is stern and serious as he carefully reviews the line of cadets.

It is getting worse for Sir Rat. He stumbles to his right and bumps into Moses, who pushes him back up. The boy, delirious now, mumbles, "I got it. I'm good," and struggles to straighten up.

John takes it all in, purses his lips, and scowls.

Inevitably, Sir Rat's head wobbles one last time, his eyes roll back in his head, and the young cadet passes out, collapsing sideward onto the ground with a heavy thunk next to his musket.

Old Spex and the rest of the reviewing crowd hear the noise and sense that something has gone amiss, but the front ranks of cadets block the view. And in the ranks, the cover up begins. Sam passes off his rifle to Garland and slips down to huddle over Sir Rat. He's quickly joined by Duck, and both stay low to remain hidden inside the formation so Old Spex and other observers don't see.

Cadet Jack Stanard, standing in a front rank, steps forward, musket in the vertical carry position against his left shoulder. Stanard salutes the superintendent with his right hand against the musket and forcefully sounds off on behalf of the battalion.

"Sir, the battalion is formed and ready. All cadets are present or accounted for, Sir."

Old Spex proudly returns the salute, and the crowd applauds.

But inside the ranks, and still staying low so they won't be detected, not everyone is formed and ready. Duck and Sam pick Sir Rat up by the arms and ankles and carry him to the outside and back of the formation. Moses and John maintain stiff body position as their eyes track down and observe the careful extraction of Sir Rat. Duck and Sam carry the now delirious Sir Rat behind the formation and toward the nearby residence.

Girls' Boarding House

Duck and Sam look back nervously to make sure they haven't been observed. Sir Rat's eyes are rolled back in his head.

As Duck and Sam approach the porch of the house adjacent to the school, the young girls gathered on the lawn in front of the house to observe the battalion's exercises scatter to get clear a path for the boys.

The two girls in bonnets who were sipping drinks get up from the bench as Duck and Sam, carrying the unconscious Sir Rat, approach. The boys hastily arrange Sir Rat on the bench as they prop his back and head up against one of the arms and lift his legs onto the bench. Duck is left to steady Sir Rat with one hand to keep him from falling off the bench and holds Sir Rat's hat in the other hand as Sam heads for the door.

Urgently, Sam twists the mechanical doorbell ringer. Once, twice, three times it rings with no response. He then knocks on the door, increasingly frustrated when no one answers. Stymied, he turns back to Duck to express his chagrin when, at that very moment, the front door cracks open. The moment Sam turns back around, everything changes for the young man.

Libby Clinedinst, dark hair swept back to reveal intelligent, piercing blue eyes, stares back at him. Stunned by her beauty and her sudden apparition, Sam struggles to pull himself together. He straightens and steps back from the doorway.

"Uh, we … uh," he mumbles. It's all he can manage.

Libby looks at him curiously. Watching him stutter, she remains utterly unimpressed, impatient, and all business. Her eyebrows knit. "May we help you?"

"We … uh."

Looking past Sam to the bench, Libby's eyes land on Sir Rat, his shoulder propped up awkwardly, eyes rolled back, hands crossed in front. Then her gaze turns to Duck, who is now standing at a stiff position of attention behind Sir Rat.

"Is he dead?" Libby asks, somewhat alarmed.

Sam turns abruptly around to look at the unconscious boy lying on the bench behind him, and then turns back to the girl, challenging her with the question, "Well, what kind of a thing is that to say?"

Not sure what to make of the situation, Libby tosses Sam a scowl, followed by a look that could freeze water. She backs off, turns, and closes the heavy front door in Sam's face.

Sam is stupefied. "Uh …" is all that comes out of his mouth.

"What happened?" asks Duck.

Sam turns to his friend, confused. "I don't know."

Turning back to the door, Sam knocks again, rings the bell again, calling out with greater urgency, "Uh … ma'am? Ma'am?"

The front door opens back up abruptly. Instead of the girl, an attractive older woman now stands formidably in the doorway. The girl stands behind her.

Sam stiffens and comes to attention.

Quickly taking Sam and his bewilderment into account, the woman looks around. She sees young Sir Rat splayed on her bench and Duck at his side stiff as a statue.

"Oh, my goodness," she says. "He's not dead, is he?"

Regaining his self-assuredness, Sam clasps his hands behind his back and explains, "No ma'am."

Flashing a confident, polite smile, he adds, "Notwithstanding what that girl decided to the contrary."

Mildly offended and perhaps a bit amused at the cadet's perceived impudence, the mother retorts with equal confidence, "Well, young man, 'that girl' is my daughter."

With more than a hint of condescension, Libby's mother, Mrs. Eliza Clinedinst, continues. "We are not from these parts, and she has never seen a cadet before, so she would not know what is normal or not normal around here."

Clearly in command not only of the situation, but also the porch, she adds a touch of humor, to goad Sam, "and the only thing she 'decided' was that there was an intellectually impaired cadet at my doorstep, with …" Stepping past Sam, who quickly gets out of the way, Mrs. Clinedinst walks toward the bench where Sir Rat is laid out. With an unmistakable air of superiority, underscored by a raised, judging eyebrow, she directs the rest of her comment at Duck, "… perhaps, a drunken colleague?"

At that, Sir Rat moves, emitting a low moan.

Having fully established the hierarchy of who is in charge, and having thoroughly embarrassed the cadets, Libby's mother turns and heads back toward the front door, formally motioning with her hand for the boys to follow.

"Well, bring him in." she says condescendingly. "Let's see what we can do."

At … conversation?

A while later, in the formally decorated sitting room of the boarding house, Sir Rat is slowly on his way to a comfortable recovery. Instead of a bench, he now rests on an overstuffed couch, his head propped up with a pillow.

With Sam and Duck standing quietly and uncomfortably nearby, Libby Clinedinst takes a moist, cool cloth and tenderly wipes Sir Rat's forehead. She holds a sandwich made with thick slices of bread up to the ailing Sir Rat's lips and helps the poor boy take a bite. But as she turns aside, Sir Rat, now fully recovered but still playing along and enjoying himself royally, gives Duck and Sam a secret smile, nodding his head as if to say *the life of a Rat isn't so bad, after all.*

Sam, trying to figure out how to engage this beautiful girl, finally breaks the awkward silence. "You're ... not from around here?"

The young girl answers assertively, barely looking up at Sam. "I should say not. My aunt lives here. We live in New Market. You know, up north. Where Jackson fought."

Sam nods dumbly, unable to string more than two words together in a cohesive sentence. An awkward silence hangs over the room until Libby has had enough. Her gaze still fixed on Sir Rat, she asks, "So ... is this the best you can do...?"

Sam's face knots in confusion. *The best you can do? What does she mean?*

But the other two boys know exactly what she means. Duck glances desperately at Sam, eyes flaring, urgent and pleading for Sam to say something—anything!—to the girl.

Sir Rat looks at Sam with the same compelling expression, his eyes opened wide, trying to persuade Sam to engage.

Libby looks up from Sir Rat and gazes directly into Sam's eyes with that same look that stunned him when she first appeared like an angelic apparition in the doorway. She finishes her sentence with, "... at ... conversation?"

Overcome, he says nothing and looks away.

Duck gives Sam another meaningful look, but all Sam can manage is "Uh...."

Sam, confused and disgusted with himself, gives up and clomps out of the room, leaving Duck and Sir Rat alone with Libby.

Libby turns back to Sir Rat. In a slightly sarcastic tone, she manages to get in the last words: "Pleasure chatting with you."

The Wolf

General Grant's Union Field Headquarters, April 1864

Outside an open military tent, with the light of dusk illuminating a tree-lined river in the background, General Grant and five other Union officers are gathered around a field table covered with maps. Grant taps a pointer on the map and says, "While I'm taking the main army south toward Richmond, I'm sending General Sigel south to the Shenandoah Valley, Lee's breadbasket." The general puts the critical importance of this move into stark perspective. "If we take the Valley before the summer harvest, we'll cut off Lee's food supply and end the war."

Captain Dupont, the youngest of the officers, looks down and studies the map carefully. He holds his right hand steady on his chest, halfway down his tunic, four fingers pressed into the fold of the thick wool jacket. Henry A. Dupont is a quietly competent artillery officer who comes from a prominent Delaware family. He wears a simple officer's cap with cross cannon insignia against a blood-red background. Red, the heraldic military color for artillery.

Grant looks up and addresses the other officers present. "Excuse me, gentlemen...." The other officers take their cue and leave Grant alone with Dupont. Grant, cigar in hand, puts his arm on Dupont's shoulder and guides the captain away from the table for a private stroll toward the river.

"This campaign," the general says, "will be something of a family affair. Our first lady, Mary Todd Lincoln, is a cousin to the rebel general we're going to be facing in the Valley, John C. Breckinridge."

Grant smiles and studies the intense young Dupont for a moment. "You're wondering what the hell you're doing here."

Young Dupont nods politely. "As a matter of fact, sir, I am."

"Well, Franz Sigel is a politician, not a soldier. All he has to do is take the railroad, but I'm not going to take any chances. I'm going to attach you and your guns ... and a regiment of Ohio boys."

Politicians parading as military men. Dupont nods. He understands the stakes now. He understands the task Grant has given him. He knows it's up to him to make things work in the upcoming campaign.

The Stakes are Understood

General Breckinridge's Confederate Field Headquarters

In a simple camp, consisting of open-sided tents that are nothing more than tarps hastily pulled over poles, General Breckinridge sips a glass of whiskey and reads a personal letter at his desk set out in the open. He's still wearing his black hat, but his jacket is off and his white shirt billows in a light breeze.

Major Semple rides up on an impressive red stallion and dismounts. He approaches the desk, removing his riding gloves as he walks. Pausing to observe the general reading, he smiles.

"Your daily briefing from Mary?" Semple says.

Breckinridge looks back over his left shoulder and replies, "Ever since she turned ten, girl just won't let me run the war without her."

Semple walks around to an open chair on the other side of the desk, his left hand on the hilt of his saber. He sits and stretches out his legs. "Well, then, what would your daughter say about the New Market Gap?"

Breckinridge thinks about it. "Hum." He takes a drink from the heavy glass in front of him. "Let's see."

He squints down at the letter. "She says Grant has a big problem. The only sizable force he has available to throw at us ... is Franz Sigel. Hmm."

Still holding the letter, Breckinridge stands, moves to another table by the tent, and retrieves a tin cup for his guest.

"She says Grant knows that Sigel is an idiot, so he will surely send a real soldier along to help him out."

Breckinridge plops down the cup in front of Semple. "But, she thinks, Sigel will almost certainly take offense and resist the help." Breckinridge takes a bottle and pours a generous portion of whiskey into the cup. Semple politely accepts the whiskey and Breckinridge concludes: "Smart girl, huh?"

Perplexed, Semple puzzles through what Breckinridge really means. He thinks about it, then asks, "So then, at New Market—"

"—we break Grant's back and save Lee's army, Charlie," Breckinridge finishes the sentence and raises his glass to toast the idea. Semple leans forward to clink his tin cup to Breckinridge's glass and is just about to bring the whisky to his lips when Breckinridge continues. "Unless, of course...."

Breckinridge stops mid sentence to take a long drink. Semple waits. The general puts down his glass, then continues, "... the soldiers I asked for don't arrive in time." Breckinridge then shrugs and leans back, resigned, as he makes his point. "In which case we lose the war. It's my fault." He nods toward Semple, "It's your fault ..."

Semple, a bit taken back, does not drink. The young major puts down his cup and continues to listen intently.

"... and from the Union gallows next to you, I will surely remark ... that I told you so."

Breckinridge's smile is easy, but his eyes are steel. Semple looks inward as he contemplates with crystal clarity this image of the stakes and the urgency of the task the two men face.

One Slave to Another

Early morning lights up the front of the VMI fortress, with Old Judge's tiny bakery building tucked off to the right. In the background, two gunshots ring out.

Inside the bakery, strong, dark hands knead and roll a mound of floury dough.

Just outside, through the side window, Moses Ezekiel taps on the glass and peers in. He proudly holds up two fat, freshly shot rabbits for Old Judge to see.

Old Judge looks over, curious, yet a bit troubled. Moses moves away from the window and hurries around toward the front door of the bakery.

Just as Moses reaches the front of the bakery, the door quickly opens and Old Judge hurries Moses inside. Old Judge steps out, peering right and left, uneasy at the thought that they may have been noticed. He quickly closes the door behind them.

Moses is puzzled. Old Judge reminds him, "We already got our delivery, son."

Moses stands back against the wall, against a cabinet between two windows. He wears a gray working jacket and blue-billed hat with small brass letters V, M, and I pinned to the front. Moses holds a shotgun vertically against his shoulder. He speaks quietly, hesitatingly, with a slight smile. "This is from me. This is extra."

Old Judge carries the rabbits back to his chair in front of the table where mounds of dough and flour still wait. The older man turns back to study Moses, trying to make sense of the young man's gesture. Old Judge ask, "One slave to another?"

Moses smiles, shifts his weight from one foot to the other. His dark eyes are soft and friendly. "Not exactly. I just thought … you'd know some families could use them."

Old Judge sits down again and hangs the rabbits on a peg behind the table, hiding them from view. "Course I do."

He carefully studies the young man before asking, "This ain't about your people and the pharaoh? And you feeling something them other boys can't feel? Huh?"

Moses looks intently at Old Judge, then looks down to the floor. Unsure of a proper response, Moses feels uncomfortable.

Old Judge notices that Moses is carrying a sheaf of papers tucked behind his belt. He points and asks. "What's that you got there?"

Caught off guard, Moses pushes down on the folded sheaf to hide it further behind his beltline. "Oh, nothing."

Old Judge holds out his left hand and motions with his fingers for Moses to give him the sheaf. He speaks in a fatherly, protective, insistent tone. "You let me be the judge of that."

Moses hesitates, then takes the folded sheaf of paper out and hands it over.

Old Judge carefully unfolds the papers and looks through them. The first is a charcoal sketch of a cadet, musket in hand, looking out, hand above his eyes as he looks to the horizon. The detail, the feel communicated by the soldier's stance and look on his face speaks of an artist well beyond Moses' years. Old Judge nods, impressed with the talent shown in the work, and looks back to Moses.

Old Judge then moves the top drawing to reveal a second charcoal sketch that comes as a surprise. It is a beautifully drawn sketch of a young slave girl, working in the fields. Her hair swept up under a kerchief, she is dressed in a billowing long-sleeved blouse and long skirt. Her face is tired and worn. Her muscles appear to tire under the weight of the field tool. Her eyes are weary, her days long, and she toils in hopeless pride.

Old Judge is stunned. "Now. Look at this." The detail is exquisite. He studies the drawing for a long moment, clearly touched not only by the subject that speaks to him of his own struggle, but also the depth of feeling Moses is capable of communicating with his drawing. Fighting back emotion, he says softly, "My, my, my." Touched by Old Judge's reaction to the drawing, Moses doesn't know what to say.

Still holding the sketch, Old Judge now reaches back with his spare hand and lifts up the two rabbits. "Well, then, I thank you for these."

Happy to oblige, yet slightly embarrassed, Moses manages a smile.

Old Judge is clearly proud and impressed. There is more to this boy than he thought. He holds up the rabbits and reassures young Moses, "There are some children who won't go hungry tonight."

Old Judge carefully folds and hands Moses back the rest of the papers, but gently holds back the drawing of the slave girl for a moment. Old Judge looks carefully at the drawing again, then looks up and asks Moses "And, who is this?"

Moses contemplates the drawing, its silent depiction of the times, and replies, sadness tinged with quiet emotion. "Someone who *will* go hungry."

Just a Rat

Inside the barracks quad on the ground level, a long line of cadets leads up to a table with foodstuffs, pieces of bread, and candies.

A small sign identifies it as "Cadet Store." Behind the table, an older civilian, the man who runs the store, records transactions with a pencil in a notebook. The sales clerk scratches onto the paper and informs the first cadet, "All right, that's eighteen credits."

With some effort, Sir Rat finally has worked his way up to the next in line. With a big smile on his face, he asks the clerk, "How much are the sausages, sir?"

Just as the clerk is about to answer, a commotion arises from the stairway leading to the quad as John Wise hurries down, only to find himself at end of the line.

Back at the front of the line, a voice rises behind Sir Rat, admonishing him. "Get behind, Rat."

Jack Stanard, in line directly behind Sir Rat, pulls the boy back and pushes him aside. Taken back, Sir Rat objects. "Hey!" and boldly steps back up to the front.

Stanard blocks the way with his arm. Dressing him down, he asserts, "I said, get behind."

Unflinching, Sir Rat stands up for himself. "No. I was here first, sir."

John overhears the commotion and steps forward slowly as the exchange continues.

In front, Stanard slams both hands into little Sir Rat's chest and pushes him backward, onto the dirt. Sir Rat hits the ground hard, throwing his hat off and knocking the air out of him. "Ahhh!" The youngster exhales in pain.

John, now up at the front of the line, grabs Stanard by the arm and turns him around. The two older cadets now stand face-to-face, eye-to-eye.

John points to the ground where Sir Rat lies sprawled out and demands an explanation. "What's going on here?" The two young men, jaws set, draw closer and closer in confrontation. John continues, "This is my rat. Hands off."

The salesclerk remains silent, stepping back slightly even as Stanard steps forward to put his face in John's. "Butt out if you know what's good for you."

But John stands fast. He jabs a finger into Stanard's chest. "You have no right to push a cadet out of your way."

Stanard's face tightens as he moves forward, even closer to John. "He's just a rat. Don't pretend to boss me around, Johnny." Spoiling for a fight, Stanard takes it to the next level and begins to mock John, making fun of him in front of the other cadets.

"Wasn't it your father, the 'governor'…" Stanard looks back over his shoulder, making sure the other cadets can hear his insult "…who opposed secession?" A laugh or two breaks out in the crowd. Stanard hits home, adding, "The old fool."

With that, John shoves his erstwhile friend backwards, but Stanard catches himself and pushes John right back. John has had enough. He comes back with a surprise right cross with his fist, hard to Stanard's jaw.

Stunned, Stanard falls back into the crowd of cadets, who jump forward to hold the two struggling fighters apart. Sir Rat is on his feet and is now among those containing the fight.

A bell rings out and keeps ringing. Stanard's hat is off, his hair is disheveled, his lower lip is bloody. Another cadet has an arm across Stanard's chest, pulling him back as two other cadets drag John back, but both boys are eager for a fight and strain to get back at one another.

"Come on!" John shouts.

From the floor above, Captain Chinook and another uniformed faculty officer rush forward to the banister and look down on the melee. Chinook points down at the crowd and shouts.

"Gentlemen, stand fast! You're all under arrest!" Chinook then rushes for the stairs leading down to the quad.

Stanard breaks free, wipes the blood from his mouth, and shouts, "This ain't over, Johnny."

In answer, John strains forward, menacing. "You bet it ain't."

A cadet nearby shouts, "Come on, we got to go!" as Staff Officer Chinook heads down the stairs, shouting, "Hey!"

Cadets scatter in all directions. Jack Stanard and John Wise face one another for a single instant, then turn and head away in opposite directions just as Chinook reaches the barrels at the end of the stairway, quickly crossing the quad toward the store.

By the time Chinook arrives, frustrated and clearly annoyed, the place is deserted except for the salesclerk.

General Franz Sigel

Union General Franz Sigel's Temporary Headquarters, Winchester, Virginia

Embodying importance and wealth, the stately brick mansion, framed with high trees and ringed with steel fence posts and brick pillars is an impressive site for Union General Franz Sigel's Temporary Headquarters. White eagle sculptures top the two stone pillars at the entrance to the grounds, guarded by armed Union sentries in dress blue uniforms. Inside the well-kept grounds, officers on horseback pass by as other officers ascend steps leading up to the formal front entryway of the mansion where more armed guards stand watch.

Inside, General Sigel, well-known New York politician-turned-general, comes down the staircase from the upper floor, passing ornate paintings on the walls. Sigel holds a map in his left hand and a pipe to his mouth with his right hand.

At the base of the staircase, Captain Henry Dupont dutifully waits. Dupont bows respectfully, then delivers the proper military greeting.

"General Sigel. My respects."

A pompous man of German descent, Sigel gives Dupont a cursory up and down look as he continues across the hallway to another room. As the general passes, Dupont continues to introduce himself, explaining as he goes.

"I have the honor of providing artillery support—" Sigel, followed by an aide, quickly brushes by the junior captain without the merest acknowledgement of his presence. Dupont turns to follow and continues speaking, now to the general's back. "—for your advance."

Dupont walks past more guards at a doorway and enters a formal drawing room filled with well-dressed staff officers standing stiffly and waiting for the general. With his back still to Dupont, General Sigel finally acknowledges his visitor in a distinct German accent. "Welcome, dear Captain Dupont."

Sigel moves around a table, passing in front of the fireplace where two officers wait at attention, and takes his position in a well-lit alcove. The welcome Dupont receives is cold and formal. "You have been sent by General Grant to spy on us, yes?"

Smug and dismissive, Sigel looks down at his papers and puffs on his pipe.

Dupont stands at a proper but relaxed position of attention and responds respectfully to reassure the general "I wish only to provide the best possible support for *your* command, sir."

The room is deathly still.

"Are there any maps of the route?" Dupont's voice is calm and controlled.

At that, an aide approaches Sigel with a map mounted on a wooden board. Sigel waves him away with his hand as Dupont continues "Any intelligence of the enemy dispositions … or intentions?"

Sigel, his eyes cold and dismissive and his contempt for the younger man tangible, finally looks up. He stares at Dupont for a full moment before stepping toward him. Dupont stiffens to a more formal position of attention, as Sigel draws, menacingly close, to within a foot of Dupont's face.

Sigel's face tightens with icy disdain. "General Grant is your patron. Let him provide whatever you need." Sigel holds the look to let it sink in and then turns and moves back into his alcove, leaving Dupont to endure the abuse, standing in silence.

Love at First Sight

Sam Atwill paces back and forth outside the boarding house, his brow knit in concentration as he mutters under his breath. Behind him, the horizon is bathed in a soft, soothing, purple light, but his full dress uniform—plumed hat, starched white trousers, and smart, fitted jacket with brass buttons glinting in the twilight—are anything but soothing.

His hat bobs up and down as he paces. "I need to tell you something. When I first saw you …" He struggles for the right words. "Your eyes. Your mouth … uh.…" Having never courted a young lady before, the normally disheveled young man struggles to put his feelings into words.

He looks down, frustrated. "All right, and then I say, 'Good evening'. And she's going to say, 'Good evening …'"

He stops, smiles to himself. "She doesn't know my name." The irony makes him laugh. "She doesn't know my name."

"Do you need to come inside?"

Sam's head snaps around toward the voice. On the porch,

standing at the door, Libby, the object of his tortured rehearsal, waits for an answer. He swallows, stammers, wondering where his capacity for speech has disappeared to and if it would ever deign to return.

Digging deep for confidence, he finally manages, "Uh … well … I better not." He swallows. "Given my recent problems with … conversation."

Her lips curve into a coy smile. "A wise boy. Shall I get you something?"

Sam looks up at her, his mouth dry, his confidence non-existent. But still, he knows he must not squander the opportunity, so he braves another few words. "Conversation would be nice."

Libby turns, places her hand on the doorknob, and pulls the door closed. She skips down the steps and hurries up to Sam, stopping just in front of him. She suppresses a smile and regards him with a challenging look. "Are you counting on an uncontrollable attraction to the uniform?"

I am no match for her, Sam thinks. Struggling to ignore the pounding of his heart and to keep his knees from wobbling, he smiles back. "Wouldn't help. You'd find out soon enough I'm not much of a soldier."

Libby lets herself smile once again. Just a little twist at the corner of her mouth and a twinkle in her eyes, but its allure is unmistakable, and Sam is nearly undone.

"I didn't think I believed in anything enough to fight for … until tonight."

Her face softens. "And what is that, Mister …?"

"Sam. Mr. Sam," he completes the sentence for her.

Libby starts again, "What is it you believe in … tonight?"

With a smile, he takes advantage of the opening. He holds his hands behind his back as if in deep contemplation and takes a step past her. She turns to watch him.

"I believe in something more than just sudden, superficial attraction," he begins.

Libby says nothing, but she never takes her eyes from his face.

He stops, holds her gaze, and closes the gap between them.

"Tonight," he says, his voice no more than a whisper, "I believe in love at first sight."

The ribbon in Libby's hair flickers like a candle flame in a light breeze. A moment passes and then another, and neither one moves. And then, from the corner of her mouth, the unmistakable beginning of a smile.

If This Comes Crashing Down

Old Judge reels from the blow.

"That's what you get for giving away food."

The boys' favorite baker grunts as another blow lands. Then another. And another.

In the silhouetted light of a bakery window, Sir Rat stares open mouthed as Old Judge, arms pinned behind his back by one man, is pummeled by another. On his way to deliver two rabbits, Sir Rat instead flinches as Old Judge takes the beating wordlessly.

In their barracks room, the rest of the group of friends sit around the room's central desk, relaxing in shirtsleeves and suspenders after a long day of drills. A single gas lantern and an assortment of candles light the room as Moses pulls a long thread through a garment he is mending. From across the table, Duck chides him, smiling, "You should stick to drawing. That's a woman's work."

In the middle, between the two, John reads a book, listening to Duck's teasing.

"I see how you can pick up on the locals," Duck continues until a tap tap tap on the tall window interrupts the banter. More taps, each growing more urgent. Moses stands and approaches the window where Sir Rat is rapping insistently.

"Well, let him in," John says.

"I hope he has some warm bread," Duck adds.

Moses swings open the window, and Sir Rat scrambles in, out of breath, panting. "It's Old Judge, sir." Hopping down from the ledge, he stumbles toward John and Duck, gasping for air as he blurts out. "I went to the bakery. To make our delivery. And the soldiers were all in there with him."

"Dear God," John says, as he pulls Sir Rat close and looks into his eyes. "Do you know where they took him?"

"To the faculty, Captain." Sir Rat takes a breath and continues. "The one called Chinook."

John grabs his jacket off the back of the chair and turns to Duck. "Get Jefferson." Moses and Duck grab their jackets and follow John out the door leaving Sir Rat leaning over the table, catching his breath in great gulps.

They Can't Need a Slave

Old Judge leans against the bars on the window of the small, dank cell with shoulders hunched, his body haggard and bloody. Beyond the cell itself, a guarded holding room separates the prisoner from the outer doorway. John, Moses, Duck, Garland, and Sir Rat walk past where Jack Stanard, the cadet John recently fought against over Sir Rat's place in line, is on guard duty.

John peers through one of the slits in the open-slatted cell door so he can better see the man inside. Dim light from the window bathes the young man's anguished features.

Inside the cell, Old Judge slowly moves the fingers of his hands. The pain and exertion of the effort make him wince.

"Was it very bad?" John asks.

Old Judge shrugs and continues to look at his fingers, keeping his face hidden. In a broken voice he responds, "Ain't gonna be nothing compared to what the hangin's gonna be."

At a lower rung of the door, Sir Rat looks in, tears welling in his eyes and cascading down his cheeks. "It don't make no sense. They *need* the Judge."

The old man turns and looks at the boy. His face is swollen. His left eye bruised and swollen shut. "They can't need a slave, son."

Standing next to John, Moses blinks back his own tears. "But they can forgive one."

Old Judge moves back to the window and leans against it. "Oh, yeah. Captain Chinook, just … dripping with the honey of forgiveness."

Cadet Guard Jack Stanard, standing by the door, whispers urgently. "Ya'll, it's time to go."

Old Judge turns from the barred window and moves back to the slatted cell door. Stooped, he moves slowly, painfully. "Johnny. T'weren't your fault, son. Hungry got fed."

John shakes his head in a mix of anguish and determination, refusing to accept the situation. "I promised."

Old Judge smiles sadly. "Don't you know? It's the other way 'round. Old men make the promises the young ones got to pay on. That's war, ain't it?"

With tears in his eyes, John desperately grips Old Judge's hand around the steel bar. "I'm comin' back for you, Judge."

Old Judge nods in pained acknowledgement, and then John turns to go with Duck and Sir Rat in his footsteps. Moses stops and turns to Duck.

"I'll stay."

"All right."

"Let's go, boys," Garland says. Still standing guard, Stanard nods to acknowledge Moses, as the other boys leave. The cell door clanks shut leaving Moses and Old Judge alone, separated by the thick slats of the cell door. Exhausted, the old man grips a slat to hold himself up. Moses folds his hand gently and carefully over the old man's fingers, and together, they wait.

Honor is Honor

Warm morning light streams across Captain Chinook's oak desk where he sits reading a book and studiously ignoring the cadets arrayed before him.

"He fed people who were starving," John Wise says, his voice confident, insistent.

Chinook doesn't even look up over the reading glasses perched on his nose. John, Garland Jefferson, Sir Rat, and Duck Colonna stand shoulder to shoulder, respectful if not a trifle nervous, but Chinook responds, in a bored tone, "And hanging is the consequence a slave pays for stealing food."

The faculty captain expects no response and is surprised when one comes.

"He didn't steal it," John says, taking one step forward. "I did."

Bewildered, Chinook raises his eyebrows and finally looks up from his book. Then Chinook gets another surprise as Garland speaks up.

"No, Captain." The lanky cadet steps forward. "It was I."

Sir Rat steps forward. "I did it, sir."

Then Duck. "I did it, sir."

In the shadowed corner of the room, Jack Stanard, in his full dress uniform, stands at attention at his post, watching silently. Chinook doesn't have a chance to react before John speaks up again.

"And I bring the confession of Moses Ezekiel. So, it's to be five gallows, then? Shall I organize a detail to assist the hangman?"

Clearly provoked, Chinook snaps the book shut and yanks off his spectacles. "You know very well you won't be hanged." He looks at the boys, anger and frustration written across his face. "But are you so willing to end your careers?" He fumes as he moves his searing glare down the line of cadets.

John is unfazed. "With all due respect, sir, who would offer a career to five dishonorable men?" The other cadets in line look to John as he continues. "What satisfaction could such a life bring?"

Chinook turns to Duck. "You, too, Colonna?"

Duck nods with conviction.

Chinook turns to the next Cadet. "Jefferson?"

Garland also nods confidently, then Duck speaks out. "Honor is honor, sir. It is the most precious quality in our profession."

"All for one, sir." John proclaims.

Sir Rat, looking up at the menacing officer through his mess of brown curls summarizes the boys' position. "That's the honor thing, sir."

Duck looks down on Sir Rat and smiles. Nearby, even the stiffly-arched Stanard can't help himself. He breaks discipline to let loose a grin at young Sir Rat and earns a stern glance from Chinook. Stanard gets the hint, loses the smile, and resumes his position.

Chinook looks back over the line of cadets, fully aware he's lost this battle. Disgusted, he dismisses them. "Get out of my sight." He picks his book up, sits back to thumb the pages for his lost place. Then, determined to have the last word, he looks up briefly and adds a warning: "And don't be late for morning class."

The boys have won, as Sir Rat and Duck exchange smiles. Chinook deftly puts his reading glasses back on and addresses his guard, in a lighter tone. "Jack, it looks like I'm gonna get some baked bread this morning."

Stanard does a crisp military turn to face Chinook. He pops up and holds a crisp open-palmed salute, which Chinook barely bothers himself to acknowledge. He returns a quick salute with his right hand that turns into two fingers pointed at the door.

"Get 'em out of here."

Chinook shakes his head. The cadets control their smiles as Stanard, now a comrade in arms once again, ushers them out of the office and off to class.

Wharton and Echols

At an open fire in General Breckinridge's field camp in the Shenandoah, a Confederate soldier whittles the bark from a stick, a moment of calm in a whirlwind of activity. The army is on the move.

Muskets are stacked in triangles, butts on the ground and bayonets intertwined, pointing toward the heavens, with worn field gear arranged neatly in piles below. Caissons and artillery pieces are arrayed around the camp.

Breckinridge and Semple stride through the camp toward a knot of soldiers who are gathered around a fire, pots of coffee suspended above smoldering embers. Rough tree stumps are arranged around the fire as two soldiers tend to the flames.

"So … Echols and Wharton are joining us … on foot?" The general's mood is not happy.

"Still sixty miles for Echols, seventy-five for Wharton. Sigel will—" Semple pauses as they reach the fire. Two soldiers salute and leave, allowing their senior officers to converse in private.

"Gentlemen," Breckinridge says, acknowledging the courtesy,

and then the two officers are alone. Semple continues.

"They can make it."

Breckinridge is not buying it. He speaks quietly, his voice tight with tension, "If they march through the night and don't eat." He glances around, frustrated. "Kill most of their horses, maybe." Men pass the campfire, and the two fall silent again.

Then, taking a deep breath, Semple makes one last suggestion. "Well, there is one more possible solution."

Semple has Breckinridge's attention, so he continues. "We have 250 trained troops and artillery less than fifty miles from Staunton—"

Breckinridge interrupts, clearly perturbed with such a suggestion. "Jesus, Charlie. Schoolboys again?"

"Cadets," Semple corrects. He pauses, then adds, "Just in reserve and … only if Wharton and Echols are delayed."

Breckinridge is disturbed with the thought. He retorts, "In reserve … to fight. And if we have to put those children in to fight, then what kind of dire circumstances will they find themselves in?"

Semple holds fast. He responds slowly. "Yes, they are young, and yes, you have told me on six occasions in the last four days that under no circumstances will you permit them near the Gap—"

"And I won't."

"—but we need them." Semple is intent. He continues, "In reserve."

Semple holds Breckinridge's cold stare. The major finishes his point. "Just in case."

Anguished, Breckinridge contemplates the difficult choice that is his alone to make. He sees the look of grim resolve on Semple's face.

Breckinridge considers with apprehension, then nods in the affirmative, approving Semple's request for the VMI Cadets.

Revenge

Three cadets huddle near the front of VMI's Chapel, which is otherwise deserted. Sun streams through the arching stain glass windows, painting a kaleidoscope of color on the altar floor, and the vaulted ceiling and row upon row of empty wooden pews shadowed by state flags hanging down from the upper balcony give the interior an air of reverential beauty.

The front doors burst open, and Stanard and Moses rush in. They charge down the center aisle, headed for their friends near the front, removing their hats as they run. About five or six aisles from the altar, Duck sits, his hands clenched together, his face red and bleary from crying. John sits next to him and Sam is in front of him, in the next row.

Duck looks to his friends with a glassy, uncomprehending stare as Moses and Stanard arrive at the bench and look to John to explain.

"The Yankees burned his home," John says.

Duck rocks in anguish, squeezing his hat in his hands. "The mill's gone." He looks to Moses. His lower lip quivers as he chokes back tears, "Everything's gone." Moses slowly lowers himself down to be eye level with his friend.

"His sister? His baby brother?" Sam asks.

"No one knows," John says and puts his arm around Duck, rubbing his friend's shoulder.

Stanard leans forward, shaking with anger. "That there's your Grant, Johnny. That's how he is." His voice is hard-edged, full of anger.

Duck squeezes his hat hard, his hands wedged between his knees. He chokes back tears and searches John's face. "You take me … where I can get revenge."

With that, Duck breaks down sobbing, lowering his head as Sam and Moses also look down, unable to contemplate the depth of their friend's loss.

The Call to Action

By the time Major Semple arrives at VMI, the evening sun has just sunk behind the trees. Cadets sit on window ledges and stroll in groups enjoying their evening activities after another day of classes and exercises. Semple rides by the students, passing the statue of George Washington, passing a row of cannon, searching for someone.

Finally he spots a uniformed sentry carrying a musket and standing watch. "Sentry?" The cadet sentry crisply moves his rifle from his shoulder to the ready position when the major addresses him. "I must speak with the superintendent."

The sentry takes one hand off his musket and points across the open parade field. Semple salutes and turns his horse toward the field.

It isn't long before Semple is standing in front of Superintendent Smith's desk. Chinook and two other Institute officers stand off to the side, observing and listening, their bodies tense, betraying unease with the outsider.

Old Spex sits at his desk. He looks down at the dispatch as Semple explains.

"We do not expect General Sigel's forces to proceed south through the valley at best speed, but if they do—"

The elderly superintendent raises a hand to cut him short. "I understand." He pauses. "Of course."

The superintendent writes on a paper with a quill pen, officially acknowledging and accepting the written orders. Old Spex then puts the quill back in the ink well, folds the paper, and rises stiffly to hand it back to Semple, saying simply, "Thank you, Major."

Semple salutes and departs. Old Spex slowly eases back into his chair. Unable to wait any longer, Chinook paces forward from his waiting position to the front of the superintendent's desk. Old Spex hands Chinook a copy of the dispatch. Chinook takes it, looks at it briefly, his face signaling his distaste.

"Will two hundred-odd boys really make a difference? Is the situation really that dire?"

The old man responds, his voice faltering but confident, "I am quite sure. I have promised General Breckinridge that you will be in Staunton by Thursday."

Chinook questions the ambitious task. "That's fifty miles in *two days*."

The superintendent says nothing. *What is ther e to say?* It is clear that the orders are not to be challenged.

Chinook stiffens to attention and responds firmly, "Yes, sir," as Old Spex turns his attention back to the papers on his desk.

Orders to March

Heavy rain falls as Chinook and two staff officers step forward into the main barracks quadrangle. A bearded officer on Chinook's right side holds a lantern to lead the way. Undeterred by the deluge, Chinook and the staff officers proceed to the center of the quadrangle and wait as the cadets scamper down stairways and run across the quadrangle to fall in by company. Most button jackets and pull on hats as they go, pelted by driving rain.

Above the tumult, Duck's voice rouses the cadets to move faster. "Battalion, fall in! Quickly now. I said *fall in!*"

In the front rank, Sir Rat, Garland, Moses, and Stanard are already standing at attention.

The cadets look to one another, clearly unaware of why they have been so rudely rousted out of their sleep and into the rain. Moses fumbles with his tunic, having difficulty getting one button to do its duty. John stands in the row just behind Sir Rat. Lit only by the dim streetlamps of the quad, the boys stand silent and confused in the torrent.

Rain-soaked, but now fully assembled, the battalion is formed in companies, and in front of the assemblage, Chinook stands with his reading glasses on. He holds up a paper, lit by the lantern of the other staff officer.

"Attention to orders," Chinook begins. The enemy in heavy force is advancing up the Shenandoah Valley." The cadets listen with bleary eyes as Chinook continues reading. "General Lee cannot spare forces from the Army of Northern Virginia to meet this advance. All available forces from southwestern Virginia and elsewhere are hereby ordered to assemble in Staunton to defend the valley."

The meaning of these orders begins to sink in for some as young faces grow concerned, while others are still clearly puzzled as to what it all means. Then Chinook gets to the heart of the message.

"The Battalion of Cadets of the Virginia Military Institute is ordered to march, with four companies of infantry and one section of artillery, by the Valley Pike."

The cadets in formation remain silent as heads begin turn to one another. Sam's face reflects a different sense of concern as he contemplates unfinished personal business, business his friends are not aware of.

Chinook continues, "All cadets will appear with canteen, blanket, and weapon at eight o'clock tomorrow morning, prepared to march."

Still dumbfounded, the cadets remain silent in the pelting rain. Chinook concludes forcefully, "That is all."

After a brief pause, reality hits home—they are marching to war.

Garland Jefferson opens his mouth wide with elation and howls: *"Yahhhhh!"*

And with that, the entire quadrangle erupts in cheering. Hats wave in the air, fists pump in excitement, and cadets shout, hoot, and holler in an unbridled atmosphere of boyish excitement and energy. *They are going to war!*

The companies break up into smaller groups, everyone talking at once. But one cadet stands by himself. Sam. He looks around, bewildered, and without saying a word, slips quietly away from the tumult.

Chinook and the two other staff officers still stand in front observing the reaction of the cadets. After a few moments, he shouts, "Dismissed!" and turns and walks away with the other staff officers.

As John and Garland exchange a triumphant hug behind him, Duck stands by himself, rivulets of rain and tears streaming down his cheeks. The orders to march are an answer to his prayers, a gift. This is his chance. His face hardens into a mask of vengeance. He reaches out to John and takes him by the arm, turning him so they are face-to-face. The look in Duck's eyes is sobering. "Revenge, Johnny," Duck says. "Revenge."

As across the courtyard, staff officers exchange handshakes and reassuring pats on the shoulder, John goes in search of Sir Rat. Although Sir Rat had joined in the celebratory whoops and hollers, it is clear the youngster is confused and frightened. John leans over in the rain and smiles.

"Scared?"

Confused and unsure, the boy responds with a question. "Are we really going to fight?"

"They tell us no. We're going to be held back in reserve. We can't be sure." John's tone is gentle, reassuring, but Sir Rat isn't convinced.

"Is that supposed to make me feel better?"

John breaks the tension with a big smile. Speaking like older brother to his younger sibling, he makes a joke out of it. "Now why would I want to make you feel better?"

John puts a reassuring hand on the boy's shoulder and looks intently into his eyes, changing the tone from joking to serious. "I want you to stay safe. Whatever happens, you stay with me."

Nodding, Sir Rat's thin shoulders relax. *John Wise will protect me*, he thinks. *It will be okay.*

John's attention is still fixed on Sir Rat when a hand comes from behind and slams down on his shoulder. Wise rises up and turns to meet Jack Stanard. At first, Stanard looks threatening and ready for a fight, but then he eases up and takes a step back. "I guess we should declare a truce."

John thinks for a moment, then responds, "Of course."

"This ain't over, though," Stanard adds with a provocative stare. "I'm still gonna whup you good." Then he extends his hand, offering a handshake. John accepts and the two cadets are instantly transformed from adversaries to brothers in arms. Stanard lets out a howling war cry and leaps into the air, and they embrace in a rough bear hug and crash into Moses, Garland, and other cadets celebrating the call to arms.

Goodbye

Sam, this time dressed in a neat working uniform, approaches the girls' boarding house. The rain has stopped, but dark clouds still fill the sky as he steps up to the front door. He hesitates, still digesting the news. Still trying to understand how life can pivot so quickly. He turns and steps down the stairs, deep in thought, delaying the inevitable.

Inside, the house is brightly lit with lamps and candles as women and girls move about quickly, busy preparing for war. Libby hurries down the stairs carrying a bundle of clothing. She walks into the main room, sets down the bundle, and takes a handful of silverware from a counter to the main dining room table and hurriedly rolls them in a napkin.

Libby's mother approaches, leans across the table, and says, "That boy is outside."

Libby turns and hurries out, remaining composed until she is almost out of the room, when her excitement at seeing Sam elicits a smile that brightens her face as if someone had turned up a lamp.

Outside, Sam stands at the base of the porch stairs, staring off into the distance, deep in thought. When the front door opens and Libby comes out, holding a lamp, he turns and looks back up at her.

"Came to say goodbye, have you?" she asks. She puts the lantern on the same bench that Sir Rat once graced, then approaches Sam, stopping at the top of the porch steps.

Sam looks up at her and plays along, looking up at the boarding house. "Absolutely. I'm going to miss this old house."

She steps down the stairs and comes up right in front of him, focusing her gaze on him, her face glowing, her eyes twinkling.

Sam is guarded. He glances at the lighted window of the house and notices the activity inside. Libby nods toward the window and explains, trying to minimize the danger of what the work implies. "Women's work. Darning socks, mending uniforms. Packing food and blankets, of course—"

She takes a breath, then continues, matter-of-factly, "—pulling together medical supplies and bandages. For the ones who will follow. To help ... if needed."

Sam hangs on her every word. "Well, I hope you're not going to do that. It's a war, not a party."

Libby shakes her head and makes light of it. "Of course not." She gets playful, adding, "Why would I go? Exceptin' something I believe in enough to fight for?"

With that, a smile fills her face. She moves forward, closer, charming Sam with playful eyes. "While *you*, on the other hand...."

Sam gets what she's aiming for. "Oh, yes," he smiles. "Love at first sight."

Their eyes lock, and she runs a finger across his cheek. Then she lifts her other hand to his face and leans forward, slowly, slowly, until their lips meet. Sam's reserve melts and he kisses her back.

After a moment, they pull back and Sam strokes Libby's hand, still resting on his cheek. *Strange how life can change so quickly*, he thinks. *Tomorrow I march to war, but my future is right here, standing in front of me.*

Peering through the window above the bench on the porch, two girls giggle as Libby and Sam gaze into each other's eyes, lost in the moment, lost in each other.

The March Begins

Early morning light bathes the VMI grounds. Snare drums roll and set the pace for action, their sharp rumble and rat-a-tat-tat cadence fills the air with urgency.

Cadets and older men pull teams of horses into place and hook up artillery pieces. With high energy, cadets stream out, passing beneath the Institute's main entry arch. Duck Colonna leads the way, followed by the flag bearer, who runs with the furled-up Institute flag across his chest.

The young cadets wear blanket rolls across their chests and carry swords, sidearms, muskets, packs, and powder pouches—they bear all the equipment for war except experience. They charge past Chinook and another staff officer who watch the activity from horseback.

"Battalion, fall in!" Duck shouts out commands to keep the boys moving, and then keeps a sharp watch to ensure the formation is ready for the long march.

As the cadets hurriedly move into position and stop, the flag bearer unfurls his flag. Chinook paces on horseback across the rear of the formation, as if to secure its position.

A final call: "Battalion, fall in!"

The air is fraught with a mixture of grim determination and uneasy foreboding. All grow silent. The cadets are in place, awaiting further orders.

White billowy clouds dot the blue sky rising behind the gold-gray fortress of VMI. From left to right, the battalion formation stretches across the parade ground. Front and center is the flag bearer, and to his left, the drums, fifes, and bugles.

Duck shouts out the next command. "Order, arms!" In unison, rifles are hoisted to a carry position. Even Sir Rat manages to lift his heavy Austrian musket into place.

Chinook now shouts out, "Eyes, front!" He observes each company from horseback, confirming with his own eyes that they are ready to move out. He rises up in the saddle, and his voice booms into the silence.

"Battalion of Cadets, Virginia Military Institute … forward … march!"

To the right of the band and color guard, the first company of cadets steps out in unison. The others stand fast and wait their turn. Bugles sound out a lively cadence.

Duck leads the way in the first group, looking forward, focused, deadly cold.

Also, in the first group, Moses marches in front of Sir Rat, who is slightly out of step and is kept in line by Garland, who, marching right behind, gently but firmly keeps the youngster headed in the right direction.

Chinook and a bearded staff officer lead the way. The drums set the pace as the long line of cadets reaches the cinder roadway at the end of the parade ground and turns at a towering oak tree to join to the main road leading out of the Institute.

The main road is lined with the homes of faculty, and the cadet formation passes groups of brightly dressed local ladies and children who have come out to give the cadets a proper send-off.

The onlookers lend encouraging smiles to the brave, young men and wave excitedly as the cadets march on to war.

The column passes a group of children standing by a serious-looking woman holding a parasol. It is Libby's mother, Mrs. Clinedinst. In contrast to the other spectators, Mrs. Clinedinst's eyes search the cadet formation, concerned, looking for one cadet in particular, the one cadet to whom her daughter has apparently given her heart.

Sir Rat passes on the inside line. In the next line inside the formation, Sam looks over Sir Rat's head to the ladies, also looking for someone in particular. His eyes search desperately for her.

Hopeful, Sam examines each face among the women with parasols waving and smiling, but none is the one he longs to see. Finally, Sam's gaze falls upon a woman he recognizes as Libby's mother. Their eyes meet, and in answer to Sam's silent question, Mrs. Clinedinst shakes her head. Disappointed, Sam understands what she is saying. He turns his head away from the woman, looking forward and down. The march continues.

Sam trudges on, eyes forward, saddened. He never looks at the crowd again. The women, children, and townspeople continue to wave with their hands and handkerchiefs. Mrs. Clinedinst keeps her eyes on Sam as he passes by.

At the end of the formation, bringing up the rear behind the last artillery piece, is a covered supply wagon, drawn by two horses.

Old Judge holds the reins and rides in the driver's bench next to another older man. Having made such a march before, Old Judge looks out to the crowd with knowing eyes. The festive spirit washes over him but does not touch him, and his eyes betray a sense of sadness, his heart filled with apprehension.

All Due Respect

Inside the formal dining room of the palatial southern estate General Sigel has commandeered as his headquarters, Union officers gather around the long table studying maps. Thunderous rain streams down the windows while outside Union sentries guard the front gate as the heavy rain soaks them to the bone.

General Franz Sigel stands tense, coiled, and menacing on one side of the table. Lightning flashes against the window, followed shortly by the angry crack of thunder.

"Why is the answer 'no' insufficient for you?" Sigel faces Captain Dupont, who stands at attention on the opposite side of the table, hat in hand. Sigel's fury is reflected in his red face as he angrily berates the captain.

Dupont attempts to reply. "General, with all respect—"

"There is no respect!" Sigel shouts over the top of an ornate candelabra. "Not in your face, your words ..." The general pauses before continuing in a lower tone, practically spitting his words. "There is no respect in you." Then, as if zeroing in for the kill, to properly put

Dupont in his place, Sigel booms, "When I am comfortable, *then* I advance."

Dupont moves carefully around to the top of a table where a map is laid out. With deliberation, he leans forward, pointing to a specific spot—the New Market Gap.

Obligated to speak the truth to authority, Dupont gathers himself to make his argument calmly and firmly to the furious general. After all, Dupont has his orders, orders that came straight from Ulysses S. Grant himself. "Sir, if we do not reach New Market Gap before Breckinridge gathers his troops, it will be too late."

Sigel will not be budged or persuaded. "If I advance before I am comfortable," he hisses, "that will be too early. And early comes before late."

Good News

At the Confederate's temporary field headquarters, General John C. Breckinridge looks down at the map laid out on the table. Major Semple and three other aides surround the table. Breckinridge turns and walks away briskly.

Semple follows close behind, reacting to news just received. Semple is puzzled and can't figure it out. "Why would he just sit there?"

"I'm sure there's a whole bunch of reasons, cowardice near the top," Breckinridge responds.

Semple slows down to think about it. He tilts his head back and forth as he considers the implications out loud. "And with General Wharton on the train…."

Breckinridge is not yet ready to celebrate, but concedes. "Yes, things would appear to be going better, Charlie." He cups his hand and motions down his face in a sarcastic gesture. "Observe my elation."

The general turns and looks back over the valley, raising field glasses to his eyes. Semple stands behind and observes, "You won't need to use the boys, then."

"They still on the way?" the general asks.

Semple thinks, hesitates, then nods confidently. "Yes, sir."

Welcome to Staunton

As the long formation of VMI cadets marches on the Valley Pike into a small town, they pass a large building on a hill rising above the road: The Girls' Boarding School, Staunton, Virginia.

Windows are open and young, curious faces look out. The balconies and porch are filled with women and girls, watching the boys arrive. Chinook, who leads the formation on horseback, shouts back over his shoulder to the cadets.

"Attention, cadets! The young ladies of Staunton have invited you to a welcoming social tonight. Look sharp, boys!"

Tired from a long day of marching, the prospect of a social gathering with the girls lifts the cadets' moods. In the ranks, Sam carries his musket balanced and relaxed on his shoulder. He looks up at the boarding house and jests, "If you insist, sir! Orders are orders!" With that, he takes off his hat, waves it high in the air, and lets out a howl. The rest of the cadets join in, waving their hats at the girls and whooping it up while the ladies of Staunton, young and old, excitedly wave back.

John joins in, but out of the corner of his eye, another group of women catches his attention. A group of slave women working under the trees near the roadway. An older woman rakes at the ground. Another pulls laundry from a basket. Time and motion begin to slow as he looks carefully at the slaves, mesmerized, unsure. Then he sees a younger woman hanging laundry on a line. As she turns her face in profile, he remembers the face of Martha Ann, the mother he saw at the slave auction all those years ago. The woman who was torn from her family.

He remembers what she looked like, her face filled with apprehension and fear as the hawker presented her for inspection. He remembers the sounds of her cry—the sounds of her children's cries—as she fought to stay near them and as her husband tried to shelter them from the anguish of the moment. Watching her being dragged away from her own flesh and blood, sold like an animal to a total stranger, had changed him. Could this really be her? He watches as the woman hangs a clean sheet on the line and smoothes out the crisp cotton fabric. She looks up, sees John, and holds his gaze, her own eyes unflinching but full of the same despair he had seen that night.

John continues to march, unable take his eyes off the slave woman when a tree trunk suddenly comes between the cadets on the road and the slaves on the grounds, blocking his view. Once past the tree, she is gone.

Though the excitement and anticipation of the evening's festivities occupies everyone around him, John blindly puts one foot in front of the other and ignores the hubbub. He is miles away, reliving the pain of the past, and wondering how it is that the world came to be so unfair.

Getting Ready

Tents are up. The cadet camp is pitched. Boys holding cups and plates line up at a temporary cook fire waiting for their turn. Old

Judge ladles out beans from a large pot and adds a piece of bread to the plate of a very hungry cadet.

"Bread, here you go."

"Thank you," the grateful boy answers.

The battalion camps in the shade of trees surrounding a large pond. Tents are pitched and rifles stacked in clumps. Jackets and trousers, damp from the earlier rain, are thrown over lines to dry out.

Near the edge of the pond, Moses sits on the ground, his back leaning against a tree. He takes out a charcoal from a small leather box. Across his knees is a folding drawing board. Manipulating the charcoal in his fingers, he sketches as he speaks. "You think there's gonna be a lot of ladies at this dance?" he asks.

Nearby, in the pond, the boys are washing up. Sam and Stanard are stripped to the waist and stand in knee-deep water. On the bank, Sir Rat kneels on the grass and brushes off his boots. Garland, his wavy blond hair combed neatly, looks into a hand mirror and shaves his neck with a straight razor. Garland quips, "I hope there's more than one, otherwise you boys are out of luck."

This prompts a smile from Stanard who continues washing a shirt in the water as Sam plays around, tossing twigs in a high arc, from the water onto the bank, aiming for some imaginary target.

"I know I'll be looking for one in particular," Sam quips.

On the bank, Duck sits quietly apart from the group, his hair combed back. In the background, other cadets trim their hair with scissors or shave with straight razors.

"Do you think Captain Chinook will let us Rats attend?" Sir Rat asks, obviously concerned.

Sam remains playful. "My goodness, I forgot to ask him in our last intimate chat."

John arrives late and, stripped to the waist, heads for the water, passing Garland and Sir Rat, who is attempting to tug a comb through his wet, thick, curly hair.

"Sorry, you all," John says. "I'm not gonna make it. Guard duty." He wades in and takes a place between Sam and Stanard, cupping his hands to throw water down his shoulders. "Looks like I'll be dancing with old Chinook, instead."

"I know old Chinook is known for his dancing abilities," Stanard jokes.

"Oh, you can do far worse than Captain Chinook," Garland assures him.

"Careful, Johnny, he might just sweep you off your feet," Stanard teases.

John lifts more water over his shoulders and splashes his chest as he responds with a laugh. "Well, now, that's making me mighty uncomfortable." He leans down, cups more water, looks to the bank, and zeroes in on the freshly groomed youngster.

"Hey, Rat!" John calls, splashing the boy instead of pouring the water over his own shoulders. Laughing, Sam joins in with a handful of water of his own, and Sir Rat squeals and darts away. Sam shouts out, "Go on, get out of here," and aims a final kick of water toward the boy, but instead splashes Garland, still holding his mirror and razor.

"Dammit, I just did my hair," Garland protests, which only causes the boys in the pond to laugh harder and double down on their kicks and splashes, determined to see that Garland's hair does not escape unscathed.

At the Dance

The festivities at the dance are fueled by a five-man band playing fiddles and banjoes driving a hand-clapping Virginia reel in the vaulting ballroom of a local family estate. Locals, VMI cadets, ladies of the town, and budding school girls in festive dresses dance and carry on with the cadets.

Sam crosses the room, weaving his way through the crowd, hoping against hope that Libby will have made the trip. He makes the rounds, greeting Moses, who stands with Duck and Garland in front of a marble fireplace mantle. The boys look sharp decked out in dashing gray wool dress uniform jackets with rows of brass buttons up the front. Nearby, young girls fan themselves and share a laugh. All the while, the toe-tapping music plays in the background.

Sam continues on his quest, but he's stopped by Jack and Moses who insist he clink glasses with them in a jovial toast. But Sam pauses only for a quick drink, then takes his leave, sets his glass down on a nearby table, and walks deeper into the crowd, his eyes up, his head moving right and left.

A concerned, self-conscious Sir Rat steps out from the crowd and Sam stops. Sir Rat's hair is neatly combed, but instead of a dress gray uniform coatee, he wears a gray working jacket.

"Is it all right that I don't have a uniform ... like you do?" he asks, his voice betraying the fact that he is uncomfortable and feeling out of place.

Sam takes precious time away from his quest to find Libby. He smiles and reassures the youngster, "Don't worry, Robert. One day you will be magnificent, remember?"

The same message of inspiration Sam had bestowed upon the young man during their first encounter in the quad when Robert had just arrived at VMI. "When you are an upperclassman you will have a coatee, just like this one. But for tonight," he says, resting his hand on Sir Rat's shoulder, "you look perfect."

Sir Rat beams up at the older boy, his confidence restored.

"Now let's find you a lady," Sam adds, with a mischievous smile. Sam turns, surveys room, and spies a very cute young girl standing nearby. "Excuse me, Miss?" he says. "I'd like you to meet a real southern gentleman."

Sir Rat is somewhat taken back, and clearly nervous. The girl is very pretty, but she is also much taller than he is. Robert minds his manners and holds out his hand politely. "Hi ... I'm Robert."

The young girl beams and fans herself, answering, "Sarah."

"Go enjoy yourself," Sam orders and pats Robert on the back. "Go on," he says good-naturedly. As the couple departs toward the main ballroom, Sarah's arm in Robert's, the boy manages a look back over his shoulder and flashes a huge smile at Sam.

Sam laughs, and now, with his good deed done, he looks around and continues his search.

From behind, a girl's hand reaches up and touches him on the shoulder. Surprised and hopeful, he turns. But it's not Libby. It's another local girl, about Libby's age, in a floral print dress accented by a red ribbon. The girl manages a nervous smile.

"Well, welcome, soldier." She continues, a bit awkwardly, "Can I persuade you to dance?"

Sam smiles apologetically. "Ah. No, thank you. No."

"Oh, I knew I should have worn the red dress," she says to herself, obviously crushed.

"Miss, you are very lovely in that dress," Sam assures her. "And whoever dances with you will be the envy of all."

She tries again. "The hair, then? I can take it down."

Not wanting the girl to feel self-conscious, Sam works hard to be gracious. "Please don't trouble yourself. This is about a girl I left behind in Lexington."

Rejection is never easy, but the young girl, still disappointed, but more at ease, asks, "Oh. Married are you?"

He smiles broadly at the thought of Libby. "Not yet. Childhood sweethearts. Been together as long …" He searches for words to complete the white lie, his head swimming, "… as long as I can remember."

He steals a quick glance back to the room. "I just came for the refreshments and music."

The young girl continues to stand there, still a bit disheartened. But Sam is eager to get back to his search, and trying not to be too obvious, he asks, "Do you know if all the other ladies have arrived already?"

She looks at him, puzzled, and answers, "I'm sure I wouldn't know."

Sam nods, not sure if he has offended her, and adds, "All right. Of course."

The young girl curtsies, smiles politely, and turns to walk away. Sam responds with a nod and a smile and returns to his mission, his face serious, brow furrowed with frustration.

Elsewhere, the party continues. Groups of young girls laugh and talk with cadets. While Moses and Duck chat up a group of ladies, Jack playfully allows one girl to fan his face as he smiles. Fiddles and banjoes play, and the music keeps the dancing going. Two facing lines of dancers come in and out in a Virginia reel.

Stanard is in high spirits, clapping as Garland spins his partner and Sir Rat dances and talks to the ladies. The evening progresses, as does Sam's frustrated search for Libby. Outside, on the sweeping back lawn dimly lit by scattered lamplight and the warm glow cast by the lights from inside the mansion, cadets and local girls stroll or dance to music still playing in the background.

In the courtyard, Stanard now dances with the same young girl so intent upon Sam moments earlier, and Garland does his best to impress a young lady with his waltz as Moses and Duck stand to the side, critiquing his efforts. On the sloping lawn leading from the house down to the pond, a stunning white dress with light blue accents shines like starlight as the wearer talks with another VMI cadet.

Hat in hand and growing resigned to failure, Sam catches sight of the girl at the pond. His heart stops, clenches in his chest. *It's her.* His mind whirls. *She came, after all.* He approaches slowly, stopping a short distance away and clearing his throat. Libby turns. Her delight is unmistakable, and her smile shines as brightly as her dress. Sam's heart resumes beating, leaping joyfully into his throat.

Though obviously thrilled to see Sam, she remembers her manners and turns back to her current escort to let him down politely. "If you'll excuse me for a minute?"

The young man graciously bows and kisses Libby's hand, then departs, leaving Libby standing there as Sam approaches. She takes a deep breath of anticipation, and Sam tries to hide his excitement.

"I hope I'm not interrupting anything," he says.

She shakes her head and laughs off his uncertainty.

"I told you not to come," he teases, obviously relieved she had ignored him.

"Yes, you did."

She smiles, and Sam looks away, amused by her unexpected forthrightness. He turns back to her, his tone changed.

"Tomorrow—" he starts.

"I know where you're going. To New Market." A dark shadow of danger looms over them, but she gamely tries to change the mood. She smiles and jousts playfully, "I'm going, too. You haven't seen the last of me."

With that, she strolls away, prompting Sam to follow. He quickly catches up, and the two walk together on their own, away from the rest of the party crowd.

Libby observes, "Still not much at conversation."

"Or anything else." Sam's voice is heavy with meaning.

Libby turns to him and searches his face. "I'll be the judge of that," she says and slides her hands around his neck, pulls his face to hers, and kisses him softly.

And then she kisses him again. This time she holds the kiss.

After a moment, she looks up at him, grinning mischievously, "You're absolutely right."

"Oh, Miss…."

Being able to make him laugh fills her with joy, and her fingers trace Sam's cheek before they kiss again. Then Sam pulls back, protesting impishly, "That's no way to talk to a soldier on the eve of battle."

Looking into one another's eyes, his face takes on the weight of what tomorrow will bring. As if to gather courage, he looks down, then back up at the girl he has fallen for, at the girl he never wants to let out of his sight, and permits himself a worried sigh.

Not wanting to spend these moments thinking of what bad things might happen, she reassures him, "You'll be fine."

Touched by her sincerity, Sam holds her hand to his cheek as if never to let go. *I must be brave*, he tells himself. *For her. I must be a true soldier.* "That's the plan." He kisses her hand and holds it in place against his cheek.

Libby gently takes her hand back, and Sam watches as she reaches up and unties a ribbon, drawing it from her hair. She hands the light blue satin ribbon to him and says, "For good luck."

Sam holds the ribbon gingerly, as if it is the most precious treasure he's ever been given—and perhaps it is. He holds her gaze as he presses it to his face and breathes it in.

Wanting to return the gesture, he reaches down and pulls one of the metal buttons away from the cuff of his uniform with an efficient "snap." He holds up Libby's hand and presses the button into her palm, then slowly, gently, he folds her fingers around the keepsake. "So you won't forget me."

She gazes up at him with a slight shake of her head and a flirtatious smile. Impossible, her eyes tell him in a way no words could convey. Then she artfully changes the mood yet again, her sparkling eyes dancing as she turns away for a stroll. "No, Sam, this is the plan …"

The two walk side by side as Libby continues, building a picture of the future. "A farm. A shop. A trade, your choice. Four babies. My choice."

Sam listens, intrigued by her candidness and vision, and then laughs. "Hmm. Will that be all?"

"We'll fight a good deal," she continues.

"We will, will we?"

"I'm sure of that," she says lightheartedly. "Even when we're old together, on a porch with nine grandchildren, and our teeth falling out."

Sam chides her. "We'll laugh some, too, I believe."

She nods. They stop and turn to face one another. Libby looks to Sam, her smile slowly melting with genuine affection as she adds, "And there will be conversation."

Deeply moved, Sam leans forward quickly and kisses her. The

kiss holds, and she slides one arm and then the other around his neck. As their embrace finally loosens, they gaze steadily at one another.

"A lot of conversation," he says.

Delighted, the two lovers kiss deeply as other couples behind them dance in the evening light.

Back in Camp

Back at the cadet camp by the pond, a small campfire smolders in the foreground, while down by the water's edge, John is standing guard with his rifle when another sentry approaches and announces, "I am here to relieve you." John readily gives up his spot, glad to be free to leave.

Jack Stanard, who has now returned from the dance, walks back with John from the edge of the pond toward the campfire. "You missed a good party," he says, his words rolling slowly off his tongue. "If you ask me, I think something big is coming. We're only one day's march from New Market by Saturday night. The battle will begin the next day."

John listens to his tipsy friend's ramblings and eggs him on. "You and Breckinridge figure it all out?"

Hands on his hips, Stanard boasts, with mock confidence. "Well, I have it from Grant himself, actually. We shared a whisky, a foul cigar...." The boys reach the campfire and take seats on tree stumps. Wise rests his rifle butt on the ground, the length of the weapon steady and relaxed against his shoulder as Stanard continues to wax eloquent. "He said, 'Let's end this whole blood-stained mess … Sunday, at New Market Gap.'"

John amused, lets him continue without interrupting.

Stanard relaxes and concludes with a tempting proposition. "I'm sure of it, actually. It's an omen." He leans into John.

Intrigued, John can't resist. "How?"

Stanard takes the question as if it had been served up on a

silver platter. Confident and poised, Stanard assures his friend with something he knows beyond a shadow of a doubt: "Stonewall Jackson always fought on a Sunday."

Contemplating the answer, John gazes into the fire.

Stanard grows serious. "I'm worried about you, John. If you don't believe in what you're fighting for, you won't make it out of this valley."

Ever since their altercation in the food line, John has known this uncomfortable conversation was going to happen.

With deliberate resolve, John looks at Stanard, man to man. Firm and defiant, John comes back at him. "A man must believe his cause is just in order to gladly die for it."

Skeptical, yet undeterred, Stanard challenges him. "Defending our homeland against strangers?"

John stands firm and remains silent, but Stanard continues. "You know I come from a family of bankers. We don't own slaves. But the South's way of life has depended on slavery for over two hundred years. You rip it to pieces all at once, you destroy the rest of us."

John girds himself. Determined to counter Stanard's implications, he replies calmly. "We should not be fighting to keep people in chains."

Zeroing in to the heart of the discussion, Stanard unforgivingly asks his friend and fellow cadet, "Will you or will you not defend Virginia?"

John has thought of little else since his childhood experience at the slave auction. With serene confidence, he speaks from the depth of his heart. "I will defend my family. My friends are my family. This school is my family. I will fight for that."

After a pause, he continues with conviction, "But if God grants us victory, we must change."

The words sink in and Stanard leans over, puts his arm on John's shoulder. His voice is low, serious, as he counsels, "Keep your thoughts to yourself, John. The others, they … they may doubt your resolve."

John puts his own arm firmly back over and around Stanard's in a subtle display of defiance. He gives him a warm smile, but one that is full of grim determination. "They would be fools if they did."

Stanard releases his grip and smiles back at his friend. Then he stands, turns, and walks off into the darkness to sleep it off.

Deep in thought, John cradles his rifle and peers back into the fire.

The Language of War

The next morning, the bright orange light of sunrise filters through the trees as General Breckinridge sits at a desk under a wide-open tent, which is nothing more than a canvas tarp stretched over a supporting pole.

Major Semple hurries up, hat in hand and satchel over his shoulder, carrying a dispatch. Breckinridge looks up as the major hurriedly salutes and hands him the dispatch.

"Sir, Union cavalry in force approaching from the East, just on the other side of that hill." Semple nods, and Breckinridge looks in the direction of the hill.

Breckinridge lets out a deep breath. "So it is to be tomorrow." He takes a drink of whisky from the glass sitting on the desk. "Finally."

Breckinridge looks up. "We'll have Wharton?"

"Almost certainly," Semple answers.

Breckinridge jumps to his feet. Leaning forward at Semple, he seethes across the table, "Dammit, Major! Can you not speak plain English? Is it half certain, is it more certain?"

Semple remains in control. He answers, calmly, "At least half."

Hoping to provide assurance to the general, Semple continues with confidence. "We will win tomorrow. Because we have to."

"I didn't hear that, Charlie." Breckinridge turns away and Semple starts to repeat himself.

"I said—"

"I do not want to hear the language of losers from you, Charlie." Breckinridge cuts him off.

The general takes a long breath and continues, his back to Semple. "Victory will not come because we think it must."

Semple struggles to remain positive and respectful. "Then what is the language of the winners, sir?"

Breckinridge turns around to face the major. He steps forward, plants his fists on the desk to drive home his point. "I will lose and I will die and I will fail everything and everyone that I love … unless I find … the way … to win."

Lincoln Considers

President Lincoln sits in front of a table reading a dispatch as light streams through a White House window. Secretary of State Seward stands nearby, watching the president. After a moment, Seward breaks the silence. "The Confederates cannot sustain the losses."

A very weary Lincoln responds, "Is that what Grant says?"

Seward qualifies his remarks. "The general doesn't speak in predictions."

"Nor in boasts," answers Lincoln. "What news does he give of the Valley campaign?"

Seward begins with the good news. "We are better fed, better supplied, more experienced."

The two men move to two nearby high-back chairs. Lincoln sits first, then Seward slings his long coattails out of the way and plops down into the chair facing the president.

"The report is—" Seward pauses and folds his hands—"that Breckinridge has actually conscripted schoolboys. Cadets from the Virginia Military Institute. He is so desperately shorthanded."

Lincoln looks at Seward, words as heavy as lead weights filling his mouth. "So we have stooped to massacring schoolboys?"

Seward has no simple answer. "Only if he chooses to use them, sir."

Consumed in thought, Lincoln does not answer.

Of Slaves and Generals

With a steady clanking of gear and stomping of feet, the VMI cadet battalion marches along a wide dirt road—the Valley Pike—on their way North. In loose formation, the institute's white flag flies in the front rank, with Chinook leading the way on horseback.

A smaller dirt road, one of many that intersects the pike, is full of civilians heading south, fleeing the threatening Union advance. Near the intersection of the roads, a heavy wooden cart has broken an axle, and a young girl pinned beneath it screams for help.

Several young slaves surround the cart, trying to help. Two boys try desperately to lift the cart, but they are not strong enough. It cannot be budged. In desperation and pain, the young slave girl cries out again, "Help me, please!"

Her cries, as well as another young girl's pleas to passersby for help, go ignored. But in the rank of cadets, John and Moses hear the screams. They've been strolling along amiably with Sir Rat and Garland.

Moses points to the cart as the line of cadets begins to pass, and

John sees the young woman trapped under the axle, reaching out for help.

Without hesitation, John turns to Sir Rat. "Anyone asks, we'll be back straightaway." He makes his orders clear to the youngster. "Keep marching."

John signals to Moses, and the two boys break ranks and run toward the cart, pushing by and dodging around irritated refugees focused on their own tribulations.

When they arrive at the accident scene, John quickly assesses the situation and reassures the girl. "We're gonna get you out of here."

Moses goes to the front of the cart and finds a handhold, while John takes a position near the broken axle. Along with a young slave boy, he pushes up on the heavy cart, struggling to lift the weight, grunting and straining against the load. They can't get it to budge more than an inch or two before the load clunks down again.

Back on the road, Stanard sees the broken cart and his fellow cadets trying to help. Torn between staying in line and joining his friends, he takes one step out, but then stops; indecision—and fear of disciplinary action—give him pause.

At the cart, the lifting effort is going nowhere. Frustrated, Moses looks to John. "I think it's stuck on something."

Out of nowhere, Sir Rat appears at John's side. He leans down to the trapped slave girl. "You okay, Miss?"

"What are you doing here?" John asks. "Don't break ranks."

Sir Rat counters, "But you are, sir."

"Let him help," Moses says, and Sir Rat stays.

Behind them, Stanard turns up, too, having defeated his fear of a breach of protocol.

"What are you doing, Jack?" John doesn't want or need an additional challenge.

"Somebody needs help, don't they?" Stanard says, and the normally intense cadet bends down and reassures the frightened girl. "Don't you worry, we're gonna get you out."

Moses suddenly sees an opportunity to get the job done, and

calls out, "Jack, take this end."

Stanard slides to the front of the wagon and instructs Sir Rat and the other young slave boy, "You all pull her out." Stanard and Moses are at one end of the cart, and John is positioned near the main axle.

The cadets take a solid handhold and prepare to put their shoulders into the effort. John readies himself, then calls out: "Ready ... Lift!" Straining every muscle, they all grunt and lift, faces red with exertion. But it all seems futile until suddenly the weight shifts and the cart lifts up by inches, just enough for the girl's brother to pull her free.

Once the girl is out of danger, the cadets let the wagon drop with a heavy, awkward thunk that throws Stanard on his backside.

The girl's left leg is cut and bleeding, but it is in one piece.

"You okay?" John asks, breathing heavily.

Trembling with fear and gratitude, she reaches out and grasps John's uniform sleeve. "Thank you," she says, tearfully.

"Of course," John says, and then he watches as the girl reaches up to give Stanard a heartfelt hug.

Moved by the experience, Stanard looks into her eyes, as if seeing her for the first time. "You all right, Darlin'?" There's a distinct quaver in his usual strident and boastful voice. "Don't you worry. We're gonna send help. You're gonna be okay, now."

John and Sir Rat observe the transformation of Jack Stanard with a measure of surprise and disbelief, as Stanard holds the girl's gaze. "I promise," he says. Then, with equal abruptness, the old imperturbable Jack Standard returns. Grabbing his rifle, he shouts to his fellow cadets. "All right, boys. We got a battle to go fight, remember?"

John cannot contain his smile. His fellow cadet's tough guy façade is firmly in place, but now he knows who the true Jack Stanard is. The other boys quickly pull themselves together and collect their gear. He brushes the dirt off his hands and shakes his head as Stanard hollers enthusiastically, "Kill some Blues!"

"Thank God! I thought you had a sudden attack of humanity," John says with a snicker, and then the boys hurry off to catch up with the rest of the formation.

Five Miles to New Market

With the white VMI flag leading the way, the long line of cadets marches across a bridge, maintaining their military formation as they cross. In the distance, on the other side of the bank and reaching up the hill are hundreds of white tents, marking the camp of the Confederate Army of Shenandoah Valley in Lacy Springs, only five miles south of New Market.

Groups of soldiers snap to attention as General Breckinridge and Major Semple stride through the encampment, conferring as they go. The general, acknowledging their greetings, responds with "Gentlemen" and salutes in return.

"Do you have time for this?" Semple asks.

"If I may be asking them to lay down their lives in the morning, then I can surely make the time," Breckinridge replies, keeping up his brisk pace.

Nearby the footsore cadets are gathered around a small campfire lined with stones. They sit on small barrels and short wood benches, some conversing, some taking advantage of the moment to rest. Holding a toothbrush in his mouth, Moses wraps his tired, blistered feet in old rags.

The general approaches, unannounced, and when the cadets facing him look up and recognize the presence of a senior officer, they scramble to their feet, jump to attention, and salute as quickly as they can. With his back to the general, John is unaware of his commander's presence. When he sees Moses, Sir Rat, and all the other cadets leap to their feet, he turns and joins them as fast as he can snap his hand to his brow.

Breckinridge stops in front of the group. "Gentlemen," he says, and he drops his salute. John hesitates, then drops his own salute, as do the rest of the group of friends.

The general steps forward and offers his hand to John, the closest cadet to him. "John C. Breckinridge, soldier. What is your name?"

John, still taken aback, swallows hard and answers "John Wise, sir."

"Governor Wise's son?"

"Yes, sir," John answers, his tone humble and respectful.

The fact that the son of a former governor is in the ranks comes as a surprise to Breckenridge. He glances at his aide and then says, "I did not know you were out here." Semple raises his eyebrows. John Wise's presence is news to him, too.

"I have the privilege of knowing your daddy. He is an extraordinary man and a very able general." Breckinridge smiles. "I'll send him a wire. Do you have a message for him?"

A wistful, tender smile appears on John's lips. After a pause, he says, "That I love him."

Touched by John's simple declaration, Breckinridge looks into the young man's eyes and says, "Of course you do."

Breckinridge, who looks up and notices that the other boys are still standing at attention, tries to make them more comfortable. "All right, stand easy. Sit down."

But the boys hesitate and Breckinridge must insist, this time in a fatherly way, nodding his head with a firm, but friendly, "Sit down."

The boys slowly take their seats around the fire, still unsure of what this is all about. Breckinridge waits until everyone is seated, then takes a spare seat on a stump in front of the circle. Semple drags a barrel over and takes a seat behind Moses and Sir Rat.

Breckinridge sits at eye level among the cadets, John directly to his right and Garland on his left. Breaking the tense silence, the general begins haltingly.

"Well, the purpose of this little visit—" He pauses. "— is because it's my fault you're here. And in many ways it's my fault that everyone is here in this valley. When I was vice president, I tried to solve this problem, but I could not. And now, good men of the North and the

South will die here."

Attentive and respectful beyond measure, the cadets hang on his every word as Breckinridge pauses and then continues.

"And I will have some difficult decisions to make tomorrow, some of which may involve you." He lifts the mood a bit by turning the conversation away from the battlefield and what they may face and toward bigger questions, questions the boys can more easily tackle. "So, I'd like to know what you think of the war and what your plans are for afterwards."

Breckinridge looks across the circle to Jack Stanard who pulls a chewed-on straw from his mouth. He responds to the general in a tone of bold determination. "We find ourselves invaded by a conquering army, whom I must consider foreign invaders." Stanard looks briefly to the other cadets, then continues. "Defending our homeland is an imperative, and I can't understand anyone who thinks otherwise."

Impressed by this young cadet's forthrightness, Breckinridge's eyes linger on Stanard for a moment, and then he turns to the cadet to his immediate left.

"Who might you be, sir?"

Garland offers his hand and says, "I'm Thomas Garland Jefferson, sir."

Shaking the cadet's hand, Breckinridge smiles, clearly delighted at the mention of such a fabled Virginia family name. "Are you, indeed?"

Garland responds proudly, "Yes, sir." Garland then continues. "Well, my family has owned a plantation for close to a hundred fifty years. So I'm defending my heritage and my future. But that ain't the whole of it." With heightened intensity, Garland goes on. "I believe that folks of a certain class have a heavy responsibility. We must use our position to see that the common folk among us are cared for."

The phrase strikes a chord of humor among the cadets. Even Stanard smiles and shifts the straw in his mouth. Lightheartedly, Breckinridge responds to Garland, "Well, we common folk surely do appreciate that."

A smattering of laughter breaks out, and Garland jumps in to explain himself, "Well, I meant no offense, sir."

"None taken," Breckinridge reassures him. "Your good heart does you credit, soldier."

Garland smiles and nods, satisfied, and Breckinridge looks around. "Who's next?" He looks across the circle to Sam. "Young man?"

With a faintly pained expression, Sam begins. "I think war is stupid and cruel." He pauses to reflect, then continues, "… and nowhere near as necessary as those who are leading the fighting like to tell themselves."

Breckinridge is impressed and surprised by Sam's directness and honesty. "I see. And do you think I can negotiate my way out of this thing tomorrow?"

Sam responds somberly, "No, sir. Not any more." He looks to Moses and the other cadets before he adds, with certainty. "We will stand with you … and fight."

"And what of your future?" Breckinridge asks.

Sam speaks tenderly, from the depth of his heart. "All I know I really want … is to find the right woman. Settle down. Provide somehow for her and our children."

Moved by Sam's sentiment, Breckinridge nods, "That sounds like a good plan."

Sir Rat eagerly jumps into the conversation. "I will fight Grant's bullies, sir." Refreshed, Breckinridge turns to the boy. "I thank you."

Wanting to share his own story, Sir Rat continues. "I tell everybody I'm going to be a farmer. But if Mr. Wise would let me…" Sir Rat sneaks a glance at the older cadet next to him. "… I'd like to help him be governor."

Charmed by the boy's spirit, Breckinridge grins. "Is that so?" John, sitting next to Sir Rat, smiles, touched by the unexpected compliment.

Breckinridge senses the uncomfortable seriousness of one

particular cadet. He looks to Duck, and encourages him to speak. "You seem very quiet, young man."

Duck sits silent and frozen, his expression callous, cold. After a moment, he says, "My family and my home were burned." Duck's eyes are brimming with bitter intensity, his pain palpable. "I'll kill as many Blues tomorrow as God permits ... sir."

Breckinridge responds compassionately. "Young man, I am truly sorry for your loss." Duck nods simply. Tears form in his eyes, but he does not wipe them away.

In the momentary stillness, Sir Rat jumps in again. Not wanting anyone to be overlooked, he points to Moses, and cheerfully introduces his quiet friend. "This cadet here, his name is Moses, sir. He's a genius artist. You should see his portraits."

Moses looks to Sir Rat and smiles modestly. In his quiet, unassuming voice, Moses confesses, "I would like to try my hand at sculpture."

Impressed to find an artist in the group, Breckinridge lends fatherly counsel. "Hard way to earn a living, soldier."

Moses smiles softly, well aware of the challenges he faces—should he survive the battle. "Yes, sir."

Breckinridge leans back and takes in the whole group. As he looks around the circle of young men, he gets to the heart of why he came to see them.

"Look, I know that you must be afraid. And I know, because I'm afraid. We all are." Searching the faces of the young men surrounding him, he continues in earnest. "We must all take strength from your teacher, Stonewall Jackson: 'Do not take counsel of your fears.'"

All eyes are on the former vice president and current general. The boys hang on his every word. "To which I would add," he says, looking to Duck whose face is filled with sadness and loss, "do not let anger ruin your lives."

Breckinridge states emphatically, "This war will end. I swear to you. And you boys—"

He struggles to make his point.

"—you are the future of this country."

Visibly moved, Breckinridge pauses. He fights back emotion, and continues. "And having met you … the future is bright." He pauses to collect himself and then smiles. "So you all sleep well, and God bless you tomorrow." He looks around once more at the cadets.

"God bless all of us."

The general rises and stands for a moment looking down at the young men one last time. Today they are students. Tomorrow they will be soldiers.

Help Us Do Our Duty

May 15, 1864

Before the break of dawn the next morning, the cadets are up and about, milling around a nearby cannon.

"Duck, gather the boys," Chinook says.

"Yes, sir." He turns to the cadets. "Company, attention! Fall in, on me."

With slight uneasiness, the boys move slowly into ranks, some still bleary-eyed from sleep. They begin to form a line in front of the artillery. Duck is not happy with how fast they are responding. "Don't make me say it again. I'm tired!"

Chinook looks out on the sea of young faces, and the gravity of the situation settles in on him once again.

"Bow your heads, gentlemen." He removes his hat and bows his head. "Heavenly Father," he prays, "this morning we march into the valley of death as brothers in arms. Help us to be strong. Help us to do our duty, for our mothers, for our fathers, for our sisters, and for our brothers. Wherever they may be. Amen."

The boys look up and place their hats back on their head.

Chinook steps forward and leans into Duck, looking him straight in the eye. "Form 'em up and move 'em out."

Grim-faced, Duck responds immediately, turning to the cadets and shouting, "Company, fall in! On me!"

Comrades in Arms

As the sun breaks over the horizon, the cadets march silently in formation down a dirt roadway. Each boy is deep in his own thoughts, wondering what might lie ahead and how he might acquit himself on the battlefield. Wondering if he will still be standing when the sun sets. No one jokes with a friend. No one says a word. The clank of equipment and clomp of boots on the ground are the only sounds that fill the air. Chinook passes first on horseback, followed by the flag, and then by the long line of cadets. Duck calls cadence for the march in a lowered voice. "Left, right, left, right, left…."

They march past a unit of veteran Confederate soldiers who stand on the side of the roadway. Some, having just finished their breakfasts, puff on pipes, engage in rough banter, or simply lean on their rifles and gawk as if the line of boys just magically appeared in the roadway. Bearded and rough, a few regard the cadets with amusement, some even with open derision.

"Looky here! You boys babes in arms?" one soldier, teeth stained with tobacco and wearing a scruffy beard, hollers at them. "You boys want a sugar rag to suck on?"

Duck looks at the older men with disdain, and anger at the insulting banter flashes in Stanard's eyes.

The veterans grin and enjoy the wisecracks. One man calls out, "Does your mommy know you snuck out so early in the morning?" The men around him laugh as another cradles his musket in his arms like a baby. He rocks it back and forth, singing: "Go to sleep, go to sleep, little darling, my baby."

"Poor little boys, little ol' boys!" his buddy chimes in, and laughter erupts throughout.

The cadets look over but say nothing in response. What is there to say? They are there to follow orders just the same as the older men. They are there to fight and die just the same as the older men. They are there to do their duty, just as the older men. They ignore the taunts and teasing and, focused, continue to march in cadence, passing the veterans in silence.

Beneath a glowering sky, they march on, every step taking them nearer the battlefield. Soon the heavens open and still the boys march, now through the muck and the mud, drenched in the steady downpour.

The flag bearer holds the flag partially furled, his hand gripping the soaked fabric and holding it close to the pole. Sam looks up at the sky and blinks from the rain. Next to him, Duck's face remains cold, focused, emotionless, and, just behind them, John and Moses, Garland and Sir Rat, continue to put one foot in front of the other. Row after row of cadets march. And behind them all, bringing up the end of the formation, Old Judge holds the reins of the supply wagon, his knowing eyes full of sadness and foreboding.

The Forces Gather

At last the boys arrive in the New Market area. Even though they are so close to the Union encampment, they do not realize the size of the army that awaits the Confederates. Row upon row of white tents, worn and stained by years of field use, line the ridge and slopes beyond the tranquility of the town. Horses are corralled nearby, ready to be saddled and ridden into the fray. Behind the Union position to the northeast, the critical New Market Gap yawns peacefully at the sky.

An American flag flying over one particular stained tent announces the location of the Union headquarters. A rider gallops across a line of artillery pieces being moved into position for the coming battle. He wears the blue uniform of a Union officer. Captain Henry Dupont, wearing the blue uniform of a Union, officer guides his mount through the groups of moving foot soldiers to make his way to the vantage point where he can look out over the full expanse of the valley. Followed by three aides, he pulls his horse to a sudden halt and surveys the landscape before him. It appears that the terrain will require the Confederates who oppose this position to attack uphill. DuPont and the Union Army have the advantage of the terrain.

Dupont scans the battlefield with the knowing look of an experienced officer. He reaches out a hand, urgently motioning for a set of binoculars from his aide. The aide quickly hands the field glasses to his superior, who removes the covers from the lenses with the smooth inattention of long practice and lifts the glasses to his eyes, looking south. His body tenses at what he sees.

Before him lies the bucolic setting for generations of productive farming, where for a century and more southern families have tilled the rich bottom land to raise their crops and their children in peaceful isolation. Now this green haven is being prepared for a very different purpose. In the distance, Dupont sees dust rising on one of many hills, and beneath it the movement of many men. He can tell by the color of the air that they are moving heavy equipment. He is watching the lead elements of the enemy as they move into position, preparing for the battle to come.

Dupont turns to the aide. "Confederate infantry already?"

The young man explains, "Sir, General Breckinridge has arrived with units of the Virginia cavalry, forming south of the village of New Market."

Dupont turns to the officer on his right. "Bring the 34th Massachusetts forward from their defensive positions." His tone is pressing and decisive. He points out toward the mountain as he orders. "Get the cavalry to go east, toward that mountain."

On the opposite side of the same valley, John C. Breckinridge is also on horseback. The general snaps binoculars up to his eyes. He looks to the north and to the east, at the same section of the valley and at the same mountain Dupont is surveying.

What he sees in the foreground is a broad field in cultivation, and across his line of advance, a serious potential disruption to a controlled attack: a farmhouse and its line of split-rail fencing that encloses an orchard. This private farm is in the direct line of fire for his plans to attack Dupont's artillery being positioned on the hill just beyond the farm. Slightly farther eastward, to his right, he sees the Valley Pike roadway running north and south, bordering the little farm. It, too, is fenced. He knows that fencing slows an advance while offering only scant and momentary cover for his men.

Major Semple rides up to Breckinridge's left.

"Where is Echols?" Breckinridge asks.

"He's getting into position."

"Cavalry probes?"

"Already commenced."

"The reserve units?"

"All in position," Semple answers. "Including the cadets."

Breckinridge pauses.

He lowers his binoculars. "I want those boys in the very rear. You understand?" His tone makes it clear he is not to be questioned. "I want them protected."

"Of course they are," Semple reassures his commanding officer.

The general lifts the binoculars to his eyes again and sees that both armies are moving. Activity has increased as both the Blue and the Gray form across the valley from opposite sides.

The Battle of New Market

Wake Up, Yankees!

The crackle of musket fire echoes in the distance. Breckinridge is on horseback behind one of his own cannons. Confederate soldiers move quickly and expertly as they load the heavy field piece. One soldier shoves a ram down the barrel to pack the finished charge. The loading team hurriedly takes practiced positions around the gun.

Breckinridge looks down the line. "Everybody ready?"

Satisfied, he now looks out at the Union forces and gives the command. "Fire!"

The fuse is lit, and a ball explodes out of the barrel as the cannon recoils in a cloud of smoke.

Both Semple and Breckinridge keep their binoculars to their eyes in order to spot the impact of the ball. They observe as the fused round impacts the ground and explodes among the Union soldiers. The accuracy of this first shot pleases Breckinridge, as he continues to observe the enemy's scramble on the distant hill. He knows that all such activity can reveal his enemy's intentions, and often, his limitations, too. He mutters a grim taunt.

"Wake up, Yankees. Time for breakfast."

More Confederate cannons join the barrage and fire at random.

Through his field glasses, Semple watches as violent explosions and geysers of earth blossom along the distant Union line.

Shirley's Hill

On the backside of one of the many hills in the rear of the Confederate line, the battalion of cadets moves forward slowly in two lines abreast.

They remain well behind Wharton's brigade, which is advancing in an informal gaggle in front of them. The older veterans carry their muskets across their shoulders or loosely at their sides, keeping a more open formation than the cadets have been taught; the experienced soldiers understand the need to scatter at a moment's notice because of a shouted order or the wind-splitting sound of an approaching cannon shot.

In contrast, the cadets remain in tight field manual formation, shoulders back, rifles at the regulation "port arms" position, with the familiar white Institute flag, their guidon, carried by a cadet in the center of the formation.

The cadets have kept close enough behind Wharton's men that smoke from the action wafts over them as they wait for orders. All across the battlefield, they can see other lines of Confederate soldiers advance, rifles and swords at the carry, moving toward assigned positions.

Still protected by the crest, Wharton's veterans continue to move cautiously forward and up the hill, with the cadets well behind but following slowly.

Chinook rides behind the line of cadets on horseback. He comes to a stop, then calls out, "Halt!" When they do, he shouts out the next order, "Strip off loose gear and prepare to march."

The cadets hurriedly comply. They rest their rifles on the ground and take off their hats and drop their packs and other bags to the ground. They pull their blanket bedrolls over their heads and drop them, too.

John pulls a striped clothing bag over his head, then turns to help Sir Rat with a canteen. The cadets work quickly and silently. They can hear and smell the battle, and their faces are etched with mounting uncertainty. To the east they can see the movement of Confederate men advancing into the unknown action that rages on the other side of their hill.

Bushong's Hill

Opposite the cadets' protective hill, known as Shirley's Hill, with a mile of gently sloping lowland between them, Dupont has mounted three Union artillery pieces to hold his position on Bushong's Hill. This hill is named for the family who owns it, along with the little farmhouse and orchard that lies between the two armies. It is the position from which Captain Dupont focuses his attention on Wharton's brigade as it crests Shirley's Hill.

Dupont is troubled by the weight of Confederate cannon fire in support of a greater mass of southern soldiers than he had been led to expect. Now, as the Confederates advance in force, Dupont faces the consequences of General Sigel's stubborn delays over the past few days and fears the balance in the fight may already be shifting unexpectedly toward his attackers. As the situation appears to be growing tenuous, Dupont's aide runs up and asks for orders.

"Captain, shall we advance?"

His other staff officers await his decisions, too, and Dupont assesses his situation with care. He has placed his artillery on high ground. It's a good position that gives him a wide view of the fields around him, and he overlooks the Bushong farm, from which direction the enemy is coming. He knows the farm buildings may provide the enemy with some temporary shelter, but they will also disrupt any organized enemy advance. Besides, this initial unexpected show of Confederate force may be just a southern gambit to draw him into wasting ammunition while his targets are too far away and too numerous for effective fire. A good officer, he makes a firm decision. He speaks decidedly to his aide.

"No. He wants us to commit. We will not take the bait."

But he is not only a good officer, he is a cautious one, too. He continues, "Send this to Sigel: 'Facing large, combined rebel force. Immediate reinforcements required.'"

Dupont looks back at the advancing enemy. Across the nearer fields of the Bushong farm he now sees smoke rising behind the farmhouse, so he can assume that the lead elements of Wharton's brigade have reached the farm, well within the effective range of his guns. Figures continue to move down Shirley's Hill and to enter the farthest fields of the farm. They spread themselves out as they advance to keep from bunching up and thus becoming a larger target.

As their movements serve to defuse artillery targets, Major Dupont knows he cannot wait any longer. The time has come. He has to act. He needs to make his shots count, and as scattered puffs of smoke from musket fire mark the line of advancing Confederate troops on the lower ground and answering smoke from massed fire erupting along the line of Union troops adds to the haze, he chooses his moment and shouts his deadly orders.

"Commence fire!"

With that, the Union artillery pieces on Bushong's Hill explode to life as a rolling barrage all down the Union line roars across the pike road and, straddling the valley, pummels the advancing southern infantry crossing the lower fields in front of them. A forest of black earth erupts among the southern men forcing sections of their progress to waver as huge billows of smoke from the deafening volley temporarily obscure both sides. Dupont's men hurry to reposition the heavy guns.

Still sheltered from fire on the far side of Shirley's Hill, the cadets hold their position. They stand firm but grow increasingly nervous with each relentless in-coming detonation against the other side of their hill. They can't help but flinch at the whistle and roar of explosions, the cries of their fellow Confederates who have advanced beyond the hill into the barrage, the crackle of musketry and whine of bullets overhead. Dirt thrown by the impact of Dupont's battery against their vulnerable shelter patters down among them.

Sir Rat, the smallest and the youngest among them, hugs his rifle for support and cannot hide the terror in his eyes whenever he opens them to take a frightened look around. Moses exchanges a worried look with Garland, who is equally anxious and swallows hard.

Confederate and Union gunners continue their deadly duel as they exchange artillery fire across the open valley. An immense round explodes in the air, throwing an astonishing, deadly starburst of streaming fire across the sky.

From the Confederate command position, Major Semple and General Breckinridge stand in the midst of an impressive battery of Confederate cannon. Gun crews work feverishly to reload, rearm, and fire all along the heavily engaged line of artillery. Semple updates his commander. "Wharton's brigade in position, sir, commanding from the hill to the pike."

Breckinridge takes up his binoculars and scans the pike and farmhouse just beyond the road. Union artillery explosions hit their marks, thrusting up feathery plumes of earth and debris, slowing the southern advance.

"I can see that," says Breckinridge with impatience. He pulls down the glasses to scan the whole scene with the naked eye. "But I do not see Echols."

Semple answers quickly. "He has arrived, sir. He is filling in on the east side of the pike as we speak."

Back on the Union side, Dupont paces behind his guns, fierce and demanding. He intensifies the pressure for each man to perform.

He screams out again, "Commence fire!"

Once again the Union cannons boom forth from the top of Bushong's Hill. One round finds its deadly mark and detonates upon a Confederate gun position, throwing the Confederate gunners off their feet, and the bloody combat between heavy guns on either side continues. The battle rages unabated.

Women's Work

In the nearby town of New Market, within hearing of the awful conflict, and in range of errant cannon shot, women work to make bandages and to prepare for the inevitable flood of wounded and dying young men. They work in the stately Clinedinst residence, an impressive brick mansion with towering white Corinthian entrance columns and red brick chimneys. Old-growth trees and dense hedgerows frame the home and fill the lawn with shade. The women have converted this elegant setting into a field hospital.

A well-constructed stone wall creates a tasteful barrier between the estate and the roadway, and parked along this boundary are several supply wagons. Their arrival is greeted by women dressed in red and white, who rush to help unload the cargo.

Inside the house, Libby emerges from a room, carrying a load of assorted linen in her arms. She walks quickly, passing other girls and older women who are busily engaged in hurried preparations. She turns into another room, passing by the main staircase just as Mrs. Clinedinst appears on the stairs with a load of linen in her arms. At that moment, an explosion just outside rocks the house causing her to brace against a nearby wall. Casements rattle and glass breaks, but Mrs. Clinedinst pauses only briefly, fear flashing across her features, then instantly composes herself and continues her work.

Mrs. Clinedinst motions to Libby. "Libby, help me, please." She dashes into an open room and sets the pile of linen down just as Libby arrives. Mrs. Clinedinst takes a piece of cloth from the pile and holds it up in front of her face with two hands, gripping tightly. Deep sadness fills her eyes in anticipation of the pain and injury soon to arrive on their doorstep. Hurriedly, she directs the young woman.

"No matter how many bandages …" She holds the fabric tightly, pulling one hand away from the other to rip the fabric in two pieces. "… there'll never be enough."

Under No Circumstances

At General Breckinridge's command position in the "dead ground" behind Shirley Hill, Confederate General Gabriel Wharton receives his orders from Breckinridge. An older man with weathered features and a gray beard, Wharton surveys the battlefield through the soft, inquisitive eyes of the academic professor that he is. Breckinridge steps up beside him.

"General Wharton. Move your brigade from your current position, down the hill at best speed into that depression below the Union artillery." He hands Wharton a pair of field glasses, and Wharton holds them to his eyes as Breckinridge continues.

"You'll be protected there."

Through the field glasses, Wharton sees the battle raging in the distance and makes out the depression in the ground at the base of Bushong's Hill below Dupont's artillery position.

Through multiple artillery explosions and the gunfire erupting from hundreds of muskets in the Union ranks, Wharton sees a grim gauntlet of death and human destruction. As Wharton lingers on the terrible scene, Breckinridge points.

"Do you see it?"

"Yes," Wharton says, lowering the field glasses. The depression at the base of the hill will be too close to the Union guns for the enemy to depress their barrels enough to fire upon them there. But to reach the position, his men will have to run a maelstrom of destruction.

"Take the reserves with you. The cadets will be in last position." To make sure Wharton understands his directive, Breckinridge emphasizes, "Under no circumstances can they engage."

While this is an unusual precaution, particularly delivered during the raging battle in progress, Wharton nods in acknowledgement. He salutes Breckinridge and takes his leave to return to his brigade.

As Wharton departs, Breckinridge returns his attention to the battlefield. The lower ground in front of his position is being pummeled by artillery impacts. Smoke puffs of musket fire erupt continuously from the ranks of distant Union and Confederate soldiers as men, both young and old, are torn to pieces below him.

Run Like Hell

On the protected back side of Shirley's Hill, Wharton rejoins his unit, the 30th Virginia. Stepping out in front with his sword drawn and carried at his shoulder, he leads the remainder of his ragtag men forward, over the hill and toward the Union guns. His veterans follow carrying the blue flag of Virginia.

Near the crest of the hill, their last remnant of cover, Wharton reaffirms his orders to his officers. He speaks directly to an older member of his small staff with the fateful words. "Give orders to the reserves to conform their movements to mine."

Wharton glances back down at the VMI Cadets, who remain standing in position, waiting in a well-dressed double-line formation behind the veterans as the older men move out. Cadet leader Duck Colonna stands rigidly, sword at his shoulder. Though terrified, he is the picture of determination. Mounted and positioned behind the line of cadets, Chinook shouts, "Prepare to move out!"

On that command, the cadets snap to attention. Standing next to the VMI guidon, Sam stiffens, painfully striving to conceal his fear behind a mask of resolve.

Chinook dismounts and joins the cadet battalion on foot while ahead, with his tattered veterans, Wharton reaches the "jumping off" point just short of the crest and turns to his men.

"Gentlemen, as soon as we go over the crest, drive your men straight down into the valley." After a moment's pause, he adds one final thought.

"You run like hell."

Then with sword raised, he charges forward shouting, *"Go! Go! Go!"*

With the blue Virginia flag leading their way into the smoke and flame, Wharton's men follow with hoarse cheers, an eruption of the fierce roar of shouts soldiers have used on battlefields throughout history to give one another courage in the face of danger that many cannot imagine until they are in the midst of it—and even then, the danger so often is an almost imagined experience, a fever dream happening to someone else.

Their unbroken lines still dressed expectantly behind the hill, the cadets prepare for the terrible words.

Then Duck shouts, "Company ..."

Chinook points his sword straight ahead and delivers the command of preparation.

"For-ward...."

Duck, with his sword back out in a carry position along his shoulder, echoes Chinook's command, his voice booming.

"For-*ward*...."

"MARCH!"

Chinook shouts the command, and the cadets, moving as one, take their first step into history. Drums beat the cadence. A stern John Wise is in position at the center of the front line march; beside him young Sir Rat, his hat pushed back on his head, looks dwarfed next to John. Next along the line are Moses and Garland, then Stanard, and finally, Sam.

The cadets' eyes are focused on the terrain ahead of them where Wharton's regular Confederate troops rapidly increase their lead as they trail their leader over the crest of Shirley's Hill. As veterans disappear over the hill, their yells become faint until lost in the din of the conflict beyond.

And still the cadets maintain a steady, regulated marching pace, moving forward according to regulations. Chinook moves to the head of the formation and marches in front of his cadets, the Institute flag just behind him. Once they enter the smoke of battle, the boys will need to see their banner to keep direction and to know where their front line is.

At the Union artillery observation position on the opposite hill, Captain Dupont paces nervously behind his group of guns. Suddenly he sees something unexpected. There are long lines of Confederate troops cresting Shirley's Hill and charging down the facing slope.

Dupont instantly understands the implication of this development. He did not expect to see so many southern reinforcements at this point, nor to find so many of the enemy in the open, and quickly alerts his battery. Pointing to Shirley's Hill, he yells, "Hit the front side of that hill!"

His men frantically shift the trails of their guns and elevate the barrels to engage the figures running down the exposed face of the hill. The guns are loaded and fired in sequence. Fountains of earth and debris erupt on the front side of Shirley's Hill, opening large gaps in Wharton's Virginians and leaving smoking holes where there had been so many brave men before. Dupont knows the Confederates cannot afford such losses, but he is nevertheless concerned at this unexpected appearance of fresh troops being sent against him.

Despite their losses, Wharton's Confederates keep charging. They must clear the open fields, make it through the Bushong's farm, across the fencing, and finally, they will have to scramble up the steep hill where Dupont's guns are stationed and silence what they find there. It is a tall order, but not so tall that many of these men, brave warriors on both sides, haven't seen soldiers fill such orders before.

For now, they must make as much distance as they can in the brief gaps of time they have as the Union gunners reload. Some will have noticed that the barrage thrown at them from the top of Bushong's Hill was very rapid and meant that the guns had fired almost simultaneously. This would give them yardage before the next onslaught. However, other Union batteries have seen them, too, and are beginning to find their range. The Virginians break wider apart and continue their mad scramble down the hill in irregular groups as cannon impacts smash into the hillside and burst around them. They run with their heads down instinctively as though running through a rainstorm.

Behind them, the VMI cadets, not yet at the top of Shirley's Hill, hear the heavy bombardment that is tearing the men apart ahead, and they can hear the frightening agonized screams of the dying. Artillery aimed at Wharton's veterans convulses the earth, and now the boys can tell by the drifting smoke above that the battleground they are about to enter will be a place unlike anything they have ever seen before. Yet the young cadets continue on, rigidly maintaining their strict marching order, with rifles at port arms, their flag flying, and drums beating cadence.

On the front side of Shirley's Hill, Wharton and the remainder of his men finally reach the relative safety of the depression at the base of the hill. They tumble into it and huddle behind a smaller rise that blocks them temporarily from the view of the Union gunners. They take refuge behind this last protective ground between themselves and the flat fields leading to the farmhouse.

There is an open fence line nearby that offers scant cover, but desperate men seek any protection, no matter how unlikely, and several of Wharton's Virginians huddle against fence stakes, breathing heavily through dry mouths.

Wharton looks toward the sound of the Union guns. One of his desperate aides lies hugging the ground. He gasps, "They can't reach us from here."

But Wharton is concerned. He looks back, eyes searching the hill strewn with his own dead and dying. A few of his men, walking wounded and stragglers, stagger or drag themselves down, trying to reach the dead ground where the others lie for the moment unseen by the Union gunners. Something is wrong. The front side of Shirley's Hill is empty of anything but the scene of destruction.

"Where in the hell are the reserves?" he demands.

With Wharton are two of the grizzled old boys who the day before had taunted the cadets on the road. They look back up Shirley's Hill as well. The joking is over now. Smoke drifts across the empty crest. Wharton is furious. He doesn't understand that his headlong dash down the front of the hill has left the cadets, still maintaining their steady march, behind him and vulnerable. He bellows, "My order was for them to conform to my moves!"

Almost at the top of the hill now, the cadets continue their steady march. Choking smoke washes over them as their line of hats appears along the crest.

Union Captain Dupont also looks out at Shirley's Hill and sees the new line of troops emerge at the top of the hill. But this line is behaving differently from the scattered charge of Wharton's men. This is a solid gray double line marching at parade and moving at a slow and steady pace, keeping formation.

Dupont can hardly believe his eyes. "What a piece of luck!"

He moves quickly into action and shouts his commands, "Load shells, two thousand yards. Give them everything you've got."

The Union gunners load frantically. Dupont screams, urging them on, "Fire! Fire!"

The double line of cadets now heads down the hill. Shells from Dupont's barrage begin to impact, throwing dirt and debris around the boys as the gunners try to find the range. The air is filled with smoke and whistling splinters that surround the vulnerable cadet formation. Chinook holds his position, out in front, flinching as the shells impact, but he continues the steady pace.

Watching from below, Wharton is furious at the slow advance. "Run!" he shouts.

But the VMI cadets do not run. They maintain a steady, relentless march even as more and more explosions surround the formation.

The Union guns fire as quickly as they are able. As impacts get closer and closer to the central formation, Wharton screams out in frustration, "This is not a parade!"

One of the men with Wharton who had been in on the taunting of the boys before now stares at the cadets with respectful disbelief, "My God. They're holding formation!"

The cadets continue steadily down the front of Shirley's Hill. The Institute flag flies forward in an explosive gust.

Explosions bracket the cadet formation, flinging more dirt and mud into the air. The boys flinch as debris rains down on them. But still they hold together in the midst of chaos, urging one another forward.

Suddenly, a cannon shot strikes near the middle of the formation. The concussion opens a gap in their ranks, throwing bodies left, right, back and forward. John is thrown forward. Sir Rat is on the ground nearby, and so is Garland. Unhurt, John jumps up quickly and helps Garland to his feet. Duck also staggers upward. The cadet formation is in disarray.

Chinook looks back and sees the scattered formation. He shouts out over the din of the battle, "Close up, battalion!"

The boys pull each other back into position. As if pulling a string that connects them all, the line forms again, with rifles back in textbook position. Pulling the nearby part of the formation together, John shouts out to fellow cadets, "Close ranks!" as he takes his own position in line.

Chinook, out front, gives the command: "Forward march!" And the cadet line returns to the plodding advance, undeterred. Their flag, too, is back in position.

Duck echoes the command from Chinook. "Forward, *march!*" he yells, and along the line, young cadets help one another.

Garland shouts, "Steady! Maintain the cadence!"

From Wharton's position, the Confederate soldiers look on in a mixture of shock and begrudging respect. Someone mutters, "I'll be damned." Another shakes his head and says, "If I didn't see it with my own eyes."

The continuing Union bombardment now begins falling behind the line of cadets, the gunners unable to guess the pace of the boys' advance. The embattled formation makes its way to safety as it reaches the protected depression and joins Wharton's veterans at the base of the hill.

From the Union artillery position, Dupont observes the line of cadets disappear at the base of Shirley's Hill and remarks bitterly, "We're losing them behind the house."

His aide asks, "Aren't they safe now, sir?"

Dupont understands the danger of having this large number of fresh enemy soldiers so much closer to his position than they were only minutes before. Dupont answers his aide, "Only until they decide to charge."

Around him, a crisis in confidence spreads as his gunners realize they are now exposed, or nearly so, to individual rifle fire. A fearful voice is heard in the lull, "But we're vulnerable here, Captain."

Dupont steps in decisively to stop the contagion of doubt in his ranks. He shouts for all to hear, "We defend this hill for as long as we can."

Safe now in the depression at the base of Shirley's Hill, the cadets assemble next to the main body of Wharton's brigade. Chinook calls out, "Battalion, halt." The cadets hunker down, emotionally and physically exhausted.

John manages a smile. He is proud of his brothers in arms. "Did you see that? Even the rats held up under fire." A big defiant grin breaks out on Stanard's stern face, and Sam sees his friend's face transformed and smiles back in turn.

In view of their relief and the fact that their shelter is only for the moment before they must move again, Stanard's next words are full of their need for encouragement as they congratulate. "We showed those old boys, didn't we?"

He looks at the older Confederate soldiers and picks out the same faces that had taunted them on the road. "Sugar rag, is it?" Eyes meet. Huffing in disgust, Stanard spits defiantly on the ground. Two of the old boys look over, suitably admonished. Wharton's vets remain silent as Standard holds his righteous glare.

Sam crouches down between Stanard and John. He looks at both of them and teases, "I can't believe it. You two actually smiled at each other."

Sam's joke breaks the tension. Stanard drops his glare at the old boys, and the three friends enjoy a moment of shared relief.

General Wharton now edges down the line and reaches the cadets. The older general looks down at Sir Rat, stunned to see the face of one so young. He then looks around and takes in the sight of the other young cadets, all wearing mud-splattered uniforms, many with bloodied faces, others patching wounds.

At the Union position on Bushong's Hill, Dupont rallies his men, preparing them for what comes next. His face crimson with determination and acute anxiety, he shouts, "Get ready. They'll be coming across Bushong Farm. We'll give them an Ohio 'hello!'"

Back in the depression, Confederate General Wharton faces Chinook and makes his orders clear. "Follow me, but keep at least three hundred yards back, well to the rear."

Chinook, feeling his age, sits on the ground, exhausted. His face and uniform are dirty and smudged with fresh earth and the powder smoke of near misses. He looks up wearily at the troubled general but listens intently.

Wharton feels the intense pressure of his responsibility for their headlong assault on the Union position, as well as the burden of Breckinridge's additional command to keep the cadets out of action. Wharton's efforts to strike a compromise with these conflicting orders has already failed, and he is angry at the impossible position in which he's been put. His frustration and impatience are evident in his voice. He stares at Chinook. "You understand, Captain?"

"Yes, sir," Chinook answers, his own voice flat.

The Virginia veterans and the cadets together collect themselves in preparation for the inevitable move forward. Several, anticipating their general, are on their feet already. Wharton gives the command, "Virginians, forward!"

As before, the older men of Wharton's command move out first. There is one last look between Stanard and the two older Confederate soldiers. This time, one of the old timers gives him a respectful, acknowledging nod.

Among the cadets, shouts of encouragement help the boys get ready. One boy yells, "Come on boys … let's go." Another hollers, "All right, come on, boys, saddle up."

The cadets watch the backs of the older Confederates as they deploy toward the Union line, over the shallow rise that has protected them for what seems only a few brief moments, and move forward in a running crouch across the Bushong fields toward the protection of the farm buildings.

The second phase of the assault has begun.

Chinook takes charge of the cadets.

"Battalion, prepare to advance."

The cadets encourage one another. A voice is heard helping a fellow cadet, "Come on, now," and as they take their first steps forward, John puts a companionable arm on Stanard's shoulder.

The Pennsylvania Boys

Across the valley to their right the mass of Confederate infantry gradually advances in fits and starts toward the Union lines, taking available cover and seizing advantage during lulls in the enemy's firing.

Farther down the Union lines, a young Federal officer with a blue wool cap pushed back on his head races down the skirmish line where his men are emplaced. He looks with concern at a long line of Confederate soldiers coming toward his section of the Union position. The young officer rallies his men with a confident command. He gestures toward his men by section. "First and second ranks, ready!"

His men make up the 54th Pennsylvania Infantry Regiment, the Union's "Pennsylvania boys." The front rank of Union soldiers stands tall, leveling their muskets. Hundreds of barrels face forward aimed at the advancing Confederates. They wait.

"Ready! Steady! Wait for my command!" the Union officer shouts.

The Union soldiers hold fast and wait. The anticipation grows unbearable, yet they stand firm like a line of trees rooted deep, their muskets like bristling branches reaching out at their enemy. They know to wait. Finally, the Union officer shouts, "Fire!"

An avalanche of deadly fire erupts out from the first Union rank, and the young Union officer urgently pushes his men for more.

"Fire. FIRE. *FIRE!*"

The first Union rank reloads as the second stands, and fires as rapidly as their weapons permit.

Although the Union side has the advantage, Confederate units fire back sporadically. In the Confederate ranks, whole sections of men fall as they are hit with Union musket balls.

At his position on the hill above Bushong's Farm, Dupont shifts his attention to the battle for the valley. He sees the grim line of Pennsylvania boys firing into the advancing Confederate Army line. He grinds his jaw and grits his teeth, the pride and emotion of the moment overwhelming. "God bless those Pennsylvania boys. Holding fast!"

At the exposed Union line, the young Pennsylvanian officer continues to exhort his men. "Reload fast. Now, now, now!"

The Union muskets come down to fire again in unison, unleashing another deadly wall of heavy musket lead at the Confederates. Dupont orders his cannons to join in the massacre. They are more distant than Wharton's men sheltering at the Bushong farm, but unlike Wharton's men, these soldiers are exposed and present a target of opportunity he can't pass up.

When his guns have been reset, he commands, "Fire! Fire!" and the Union guns boom out toward the east.

The shells hit in a close pattern and blow apart a Confederate gun crew. The tide of battle is turning against the Confederates. On the flat plain of the battlefield straddling the pike road, the center of the Confederate line is pummeled with explosions and smoke.

Union cannons throw merciless fire, flame, and metal into the mass of gray-clad soldiers, blowing bodies back like rag dolls as the concentrated fire tears holes in the Confederate line.

May God Forgive Me

At the Confederate command post, Major Semple moves quickly down from a higher position to where General Breckinridge stands observing the battle through binoculars.

Semple points forward. "They've torn a hole in the center of our line."

Breckinridge focuses on the smoky confusion of battle and sees the situation. He murmurs, "If you can see it, so can the Blues."

Semple knows what must be done. Adamant, he insists, "Sir, we must send in the reserves to restore the line."

Breckinridge is frozen. He shakes his head, but Semple knows that it is his duty to the general at this instant to strenuously object. He continues, "When the Union forces regroup and counterattack, that line will divide in two! They'll pour right through the hole in the center!"

Semple pauses. Then, not knowing the cadets are already engaged at Bushong Farm, he adds emphatically, "Sir, you must put in the cadets."

Torn, Breckinridge stands arrested in dilemma. Below, more cannon fire explodes around the Bushong farmhouse.

Semple waits for an answer. Breckinridge is quiet, turned inward on his thoughts. Finally, he looks back up and responds, his voice low and hesitant.

"Send the boys in."

Semple looks to Breckinridge, equally torn, but he has the commander's decision. Breckinridge looks back over the battlefield and adds disconsolately. "May God forgive me."

Semple salutes and acknowledges with, "Sir." He quickly turns away and strides off to pass the order, leaving Breckinridge alone to contemplate what he has done. The general stares out at the battlefield below where, yet again, the Pennsylvania boys let loose a deadly avalanche of massed musket fire into the reeling, broken Confederate line.

Forward to the Line

In action at the farm, the cadets scuttle forward, their marching formation now abandoned for individual cover. Many leap over the wooden fence behind the Bushong farmhouse. Stanard, John, and Sir Rat head for the protection of a nearby building.

Dazed, wounded Confederate troops, recently dislodged by the Union onslaught, head away from the fight and stream past the cadets. Chinook leads Garland and Sam around the corner of the house and toward a small outbuilding, keeping it between them and the line of fire. Bracing himself and flinching as a cannon round explodes nearby, the three pause momentarily against the side of an equipment barn. They have successfully infiltrated Jacob Bushong's farm and are now much closer beneath Captain Dupont's guns, well within the range of musket fire from Union infantry on the hill beyond. Bullets whine pass, some missing their marks, some smacking into the farm buildings around them.

A small orchard on the other side of a split rail fence stands between them and about thirty yards of open ground to the base of Bushong's Hill. From where they shelter by the little barn, the boys can see and hear the devastation brought down on the Confederates beyond the pike by the Union artillery at the top of the hill.

Many of the cadets are scattered around the farm buildings by now seeking shelter and good firing positions. Chinook needs to keep his command together for strength and shouts the order, "Battalion, forward to the line!"

He aims his sword forward and leaves the shelter of the house to lead the way. The boys hear his voice and follow his lead, emerging from all corners of the farm. The cadets charge forward until they come up against the rail fence just before the orchard. Any fence will slow a man in a hurry, and here the cadet brigade pauses to assemble and assess before moving ahead through the orchard.

But they have halted at just the point of closest possible fire from the artillery on top of the hill, from which they are mercilessly raked by both cannon and rifle fire. Their battalion is hit hard, and almost stopped for good. The fence line is in splinters, and several schoolboys lay injured, dead, or dying. Yet faced with no choice but to move forward into the scant cover of the orchard trees, Chinook rallies them as he runs, crouching along his remnant line of boys, inspiring them with his bravery and giving them the courage to keep moving forward. Moses and Duck, trailed desperately by the flag bearer, scramble over and through the fence and into the orchard. When the flag gets snagged on a tree and jerks the flag bearer backward, Garland pulls it free and they continue moving forward. Behind them other cadets and some of the surviving veterans arrive at the ruined fence line, pausing only to deliver covering fire against the Union riflemen. Chinook, pistol in one hand, sword in the other, shouts his orders, "Fire at will! FIRE AT WILL!"

At the Confederate command post, Major Semple looks at Bushong Farm, the left of the Confederate line, almost in disbelief. "The cadets ... are filling the gap!"

At the Union infantry line, the Pennsylvania boys have not let up their relentless fire on the Confederate center. Their young officer continues to read the field to his front and shouts again, "Fire!" Union muskets throw out another mass of concentrated fire, but the cadets have advanced through Bushong farm so close to the base of the Union artillery that they have caused Captain Dupont to shift his fire away from the Confederate center, leaving the Pennsylvania boys with no artillery support. Dupont, now clearly alarmed, orders his men to fire in defense.

The volleys slam into the wood of the fence where the cadets fire and reload, fire, and reload as quickly as they can.

Chinook stands and fires his pistol over the fence at the Union line. Volley and fire is met by volley and fire in a deadly shootout between the Union line and the slowly advancing cadets.

At a second fence line beyond the orchard, Moses looks around, worry creasing his normally smooth brow. "Garland?" He calls out.

Crouched behind one of the fence rungs nearby, Garland holds his musket level, ready to fire. He answers calmly, "I'm right here, Moses," and pulls the trigger. The hammer of Garland's musket drops and fires a carefully aimed round.

Nearby, John cocks the hammer of his rifle and fires. The cadets are now fully engaged.

On the top of the hill, Captain Dupont sees that his position is becoming desperate. As his enemy begins arriving at the second orchard fence, they are getting too close for him to depress his gun barrels enough to engage them. Without the power of his artillery, he is reduced to defending his position with small arms.

At the foot of the hill, behind the second fence, Stanard tears into the top of his paper cartridge with his teeth. He pours powder down the muzzle of his musket and rams home the load as Union bullets slam into the fence, sending splinters flying.

John turns to Sam and Duck. "We can't stay here."

Sam responds grimly, "Must be somewhere a little more useful."

The Union cannons on the top of the hill are still firing, but now their rounds are falling behind the boys in the forefront who have made it to the second fence. John is impatient. He knows the men behind him are still under fire from those guns. He looks up at the cannon, and resolve floods through him. "Gentlemen," he says to his friends. "What do you say we charge those guns?"

Garland, sighting in with his rifle and about to pull the trigger again, observes with wry humor. "I don't know, gentleman. That sounds a bit dangerous."

All along the fence lines and in the orchard, the cadets fire and reload as fast as they can. The incoming fire from the Union line does not let up, even though their artillery is less effective this close to the bottom of the hill.

The thought takes hold of Sam. "John Wise, that's just what I was suggesting."

John grins. "No sense in dying if we can't sort out who takes the credit."

Invigorated, Sam and John grin in acknowledgement just before another volley from the Union side splatters the fence and tears through the branches of the orchard trees.

Stanard senses the cadets must force a decision. He yells to Chinook,

"Sir, the battalion is ready to attack."

The normally aggressive Chinook's apprehensive answer surprises the boys. "We don't have further orders," he calls out.

Stunned, John yells to his commanding officer. "Sir, I don't expect we will receive any further orders!" He looks up again at the deadly Union cannon on the high ground in front of them. "The cadets are ready to charge. I suggest we attack and take those guns before we get blown apart."

Just then, a boom of a Union cannon accentuates John's point. Galvanized, Stanard gives a tight smile of determination to John, but Chinook, shaken, has reached his point of inaction. He had probably not counted on surviving long enough to deal with a final charge, and does not want the responsibility of ordering the boys right into the hornet's nest. Unsure of what to do, Chinook looks to Moses who wets his dry lips and exchanges desperate looks with the other cadets just as Sam, crouched next to John, with Sir Rat squeezed tightly between them, shouts, "Fix bayonets!"

John echoes Sam's call, and the order is echoed down through the cadet brigade.

They hurriedly pull out the long bayonets, and the chilling metallic rattle of the action adds to their fatal determination. All down the line, cadets, from the youngest rats to the oldest seniors, make ready to charge. Chinook looks forlornly at his boys, as though for the last time.

With a roar, the cadets stand and break through the fences. They push the heavy wooden rungs away as they scramble over the top. Just behind the leaders, others charge through the orchard screaming their courage to each other. In a frenzy of focus with bayonets fixed, they run forward, quickly covering the yardage from the outer fence to the base of Bushong's Hill. They encounter an unexpected swampy area just at the base of the hill, and it slows them slightly but cannot slow their spirit as they plunge ahead through rifle fire and cloying ankle-deep mud thick as dough. The soft, wet ground sucks the boots off their feet, and with each passing cadet, the swamp becomes a churned sticky, glutinous slough filled with discarded shoes. Yet no one stops. The boys charge up the hill screaming, barefoot, and fanatically determined to put an end to the bloody destruction raining down on their fellow countrymen.

Union soldiers fire down on them. One heavy-set Bluecoat takes careful aim and pulls the trigger and sends a bullet into Garland's right shoulder, knocking him back.

With both sword and pistol drawn, Duck is focused on the way ahead and runs by without seeing Garland fall behind.

Stunned from the impact, his right shoulder bloodied and his hat in the mud, Garland struggles to get back to his feet. He staggers forward and drags his heavy musket behind him.

Ahead, the line of cadets surges forward, their faces twisted in grim, warlike determination, their lethal bayonets poised to pierce enemy flesh. Firing from the Union side begins to wither, as the speed of the boys' advance up the steep hill leaves the shooters with no time to reload.

The charging line of cadets spreads out to cover the hillside. The Institute flag bearer, near the middle of the action, waves the banner defiantly to let the boys behind know where their front line is and to show the Union regulars who it was that had weathered their artillery barrages and was now attacking them.

Artillery explosions continue just over their heads, but other than inflicting temporary deafness, the fire is ineffective on the immediate danger from the cadets. The boys' line surges ever forward, ever upward through debris and smoke. A hit directly in front of one cadet back at the second fence completely envelopes him in smoke and throws his lifeless body into the air like a doll.

John flinches as another stunning detonation passes close over his head. He continues the breathless climb, determined to put an end to it all one way or another. Every cadet on the hillside who escapes injury climbs stubbornly on as they near the top. To John's left, Stanard runs beside him, all their old differences forgotten.

From his distant command post, General Breckinridge watches the cadets charge the Union position. "Go get 'em, boys," he whispers.

In the front line, Stanard is peppered with debris and spits out dirt. Moses screams out a war cry and steels himself for what he must do when he reaches the ridge. Although Garland is behind them, John, Sir Rat, Stanard, Duck, and Sam manage to keep more or less together. Even the battalion drummer, lugging his heavy instrument, keeps up with the charge. No cadet wants to be left behind. They all want to fight side by side with their brothers.

As the boys reach the crest of the hill and begin to surround the hated artillery pieces, an unbelieving young Union officer realizes his position is being overrun. He has only one option. He shouts to his men, "What are you waiting for? *Charge!*"

The line of Union soldiers surges forward to meet the leaders of the cadet charge at the crest, their momentum carrying some over the edge and down the hill into the body of cadets who meet them with bayonets at the ready.

In the center of the line, the five friends, press forward with the bayonet charge aimed to put an end to the gun crews on the hill. On the steep hillside against many barefooted boys, the Union soldiers fight hard. Their momentum helps when they slam into the cadets, but the tide of battle turns against them as Union soldiers and stunned cadets tumble together, locked in a strange embrace, down into the bog.

Now it is down to hand-to-hand combat on the sloping grass of the hillside. Duck faces off against a Union officer, and they fight sword to sword. In another lifetime, they could have been friends, perhaps. But not now. Now it is kill or be killed.

Stanard is locked in a vicious, close-in, one-on-one fight. He dives under the soldier's fist and grabs him around the waist then slams him into the ground. The man reaches up and gets a choke hold on him, and Stanard chokes back. A punch to the face knocks him back, but he recoils instantly and is on the man's back, riding him down the slope. Finally, twisting his head to hold him down, he forcefully drowns him in the wet mud.

Another Union soldier tries desperately to crawl away from a frenzied cadet, but the boy grabs him by the leg and drags him back and punches him over and over again in the kidneys. He then slams the man's head repeatedly into the dirt with a rock. A Union officer in the melee stabs a Confederate veteran on the ground with his sword and moves on for more prey.

Having discharged his first opponent, Duck meets another charging Union soldier with a slash across the man's belly. Emboldened, he looks around, sees the officer who has just killed the Confederate, and jams his sword through the man's midsection.

A Union soldier grasps Sam's neck with one ferocious hand, trying to choke him. He pushes Sam backwards, plunges his bayonet deep into Sam's right thigh, then jerks it back out. Sam screams in pain and falls onto the muddy ground. He locks desperate eyes with his attacker and struggles back through the muck, clawing for distance from his enemy.

Standing over Sam with his rifle and bayonet raised, the Union soldier's eyes fill with murderous intent. But just as he lunges to finish the job, the blade of another bayonet bursts out of his chest. His eyes bulge in shock, but he lives only for a single stunned gasp. As he falls forward, his diminutive killer stands there withdrawing his bloody bayonet and momentarily confused by what he has done to save his friend. Sir Rat. Frozen in the moment, he stares down at Sam, horrified. Through the agony and fear, Sam nods his infinite gratitude.

Nearby, Duck is locked in a disorganized, slashing sword fight. Moses is thrown into the mud by an enemy and quickly rolls away to avoid, the blow that is coming. Frantically trading crushing blows in a violent fistfight, Stanard pummels a Union soldier and is pummeled in return. Finally he gets the man down and pushes his enemy's head into the thick, black, soupy muck until the man's frantic death throes leave him.

John and a Union soldier, with their ammunition expended, club each other with their rifles. Grappling in a clinch, the Union soldier manages to free an arm and slug John in the face, but John delivers a vertical butt stroke to the man's chin with his rifle and puts an end to his adversary.

In the struggle on the ridge, other Union riflemen remain in firing position awaiting orders, not knowing if the cadets' assault on Dupont's guns is merely one part of a general southern assault on their line. The same grizzled bluecoat veteran who earlier shot Garland now realizes what they're up against.

"Why, they're nothing but a bunch of damn schoolboys." He lifts his rifle and takes aim at John. "Kill 'em!"

Another solder echoes his call, and several Federal infantry swing their rifles at the melee. "Kill 'em all."

Stanard sees the rifles swing into position and rushes to push John out of the line of fire. John falls back, but Stanard's selfless act of heroism leaves him caught in the fusillade. "No!" he cries out just as Union guns roar and three hot .58 caliber lead balls slam into his chest. He is flung backwards as blood erupts through his jacket.

"Jack!" John screams in horror and crawls to Stanard's side. He lifts his friend into his arms. Choking on the blood that already fills his mouth, Stanard grabs John's arm and tries to speak.

"We showed 'em there, didn't we, Johnny?" Stanard looks down at his chest in shock and blood bubbles out of his mouth. Consumed in anguish, John pleads with his friend, "Jack, you stay with me." As Stanard's eyes begin to lose their focus, John shouts a final plea, "You can't die! I still gotta whup you good."

Managing a dying smile, Jack gurgles on his words. "… I can't carry you … forever, Johnny … It's up to you now."

Tears in his eyes, John screams. "C'mon, Jack! Jack, come on!" But it's too late. Jack Stanard is gone.

The pain and loss is instantly transformed into a frenzy of anger and thirst for vengeance. John lays Jack Stanard back on the ground, grabs his musket, and struggles to his feet. Immediately, he turns and drives his bayonet into the back of a Union soldier.

As if driven by a righteous fire, John parries another soldier in blue. He flips the man onto his back, then drives his bayonet into the man's stomach. He uses his foot to yank the embedded sword from the dying man, then turns to continue his rampage.

As the bloody hand-to-hand struggle continues, the men in blue gradually surrender control of Bushong's Hill as they are pushed back. The individual fighting on the crest and down the face of the hillside has stopped the murderous guns on the hill from their devastating fire into the Confederate center down in the valley, and as the Federal troops begin to move back, the Southern men in the valley, free of the deathly barrage, rise to increase their pressure on the Pennsylvania boys in the Northern line.

At the top of the embattled hill, Union artillerymen, outnumbered and unable to service the guns, fall back through the smoke and the dust, abandoning the guns to the cadets as more of the boys and their ragged Confederate allies reach the position and are freed from close combat to fire into the backs of the retreating men in blue. From somewhere amid the screams and the clash of the struggle for the hill, a Union officer is heard shouting his desperate mandate, "Retreat! Retreat now!"

Farther to the rear and on vulnerable open ground, Union reserve artillerymen hurriedly try to limber up their guns and flee with what equipment they can save from the expected mop-up. They struggle to control their frightened horses and to manhandle the caissons into position for harness.

But the cadet riflemen are unrelenting. They aim and fire over and over again, spreading further confusion in the fleeing ranks of dusty men. Amidst the chaos, a Union battle flag flutters in the wind and changes direction.

Across the central valley, the entire line of other Confederate troops surges forward into the Pennsylvania line.

From his new position in the Union rear, Dupont tries to rally his troops, shouting from horseback, "Let's go, gentlemen!" Bitterly, he adds to himself, "Someone's got to cover this godforsaken retreat." Dupont turns away, leans northward in the saddle, and spurs his horse into a gallop. "Hyah!"

Captain Dupont, who had been given the impossible task of inspiring his intransigent commanding general to the pressing need for action just a few days earlier, now faces defeat.

The Union artillerymen race against time to save their animals and supplies, retreating infantry turn to fire back at the Confederates who crowd the hill crest in growing numbers, but their defense is futile, and they must continue to run for whatever safety can be found in distance. A man trying to aim a Springfield musket while on the run is no match for a carefully aimed shot.

The cadets and the remnants of Wharton's veterans continue to make the top of Bushong's Hill. They surround the newly captured guns and further churn the earth with muddy feet, many of them bare. As they continue to arrive, and the momentum of their charge is redirected into their responsibility for occupying the position and preparing for what increasingly appears to be an unlikely counter attack, they must move among the detritus of the victory, stepping over the fallen and bits of broken and discarded equipment. With little notice, they step over John, lying face down in the mud. Shoeless feet in mud-laden trousers step among the lifeless men that came before them.

The white Institute flag falls as its carrier is hit and stumbles, but another cadet retrieves it, lifts it up again, and moves forward finally reaching the top of the hill and the Union cannon. A wounded Sam Atwill, his right pant leg torn and bloodied, takes the flag and climbs up on one of the Union guns. Straddling the barrel, he lifts the flag triumphantly into the air. Waving the muddy banner back and forth, Sam signals for all to see that the VMI cadets have taken the guns. The cadets have defeated the Union forces and have together turned the tide in the battle for New Market.

Their fellow survivors raise their weapons high, bayonets gleaming in the light, pistols and swords in the air. Their faces glow with exhausted triumph. As Sam continues to wave the flag of victory, Duck, Sir Rat, Moses, Chinook, and the entire battalion join in, screaming their pride and their relief.

At the Confederate command position on Shirley's Hill, Major Semple and General Breckinridge survey the smoking battlefield, along the trampled grass in the foreground, past the ruined fences, the damaged Bushong farmhouse, the tattered orchard and densely pocked fields, to the hill with the blackened face, where the smoke is clearing against the sky and the top is now busy with leaping young men.

Only moments earlier, the Union guns had been belching out death and destruction on the advancing Confederates. Now, a white banner embossed with an eagle and a portrait of George Washington waves back and forth, wielded by a teenager.

Semple speaks in reverent disbelief. "My God, sir. The cadets have taken Bushong's Hill."

Breckinridge, staring through his binoculars, says nothing for a long moment. Then he slowly lowers the field glasses and speaks quietly.

"Must be an illusion, Charlie. Their general told them not to fight."

Torn between relief at the turn in the battle and disbelief at the cadets' role in it, the general blinks back the tears that threaten to flood his eyes.

In the distance, the flag still waves. Smoke wafts slowly away from the hilltop and drifts like departing ghosts from thousands of black holes in the fields. The dead and wounded of both sides litter the landscape. Among the broken bodies lies the innocence of schoolboys.

The cadets are no longer boys. Their youth is behind them, lost in the fog of war. In one terrible day.

The Field of Lost Shoes

The survivors, realizing that there will be no counter attack, turn their attention to salvage, nursing wounds, and to the dead and the dying. Duck, his face drawn with stress and his thick, black hair pasted to his forehead with sweat, is on his knees. He puts his tenuous ear to the chest of a fallen cadet, listening for any sign of life, even a shallow breath. There is nothing. Duck moves on.

Using his rifle as a crutch, a shoeless Sam staggers in painfully halting steps, leaning heavily on a rifle for support. His rapidly bleeding thigh wound was not helped by his impulsive leap onto the Union cannon with the VMI flag, and now in the aftermath of initial euphoria, he winces with each attempted step. Yet he is determined to learn the fate of his friends, and in his small and hesitant way, joins the search of the field. He passes exhausted, dazed cadets, many simply sitting on the ground or in the mud staring wordlessly into some unknown inner quiet, most appearing suddenly old and tired. He limps past the Union cannon where he left the now torn and mud-stained Institute flag for eventual collection by someone who can use both hands.

Bodies dressed in both blue and in gray are strewn over the hilltop and thrown randomly on top of one another in the cold companionship of death. The flies are already at work on their pale and tightening skin.

Approaching Duck, Sam asks, "Where's Jack?"

"He's dead." Duck answers with the ragged breath of his struggle with shock. "Torn to pieces during the final charge."

Nearby, Moses hears and asks, "And Johnny?"

Sir Rat, his dirty face tear-streaked, sits stunned in the wet, black earth. He picks up a mud-laden shoe. He stares at it in his hand as though trying to understand its hidden meaning. He tries to put it on the bare foot of a dead cadet, but confused and heartbroken, he simply mutters, "A shell exploded...." and drops the shoe back into the muck.

Women begin arriving on the battlefield to attend to the injured and give comfort to any whose injuries have left them helpless. They move among the fallen with bandages and canteens of water, followed by a horse-drawn wagon stacked with litters to carry away the wounded. Among the followers is a photographer. He struggles to level his bulky tripod and heavy box camera in the soft ground before draping himself and his rig for photos of the grisly scene.

As the bodies are dragged away, their dead weight furrows the muddy ground. They are collected and laid together in a ragged formation of angled limbs. Many have naked feet caked with drying earth, and among them are young men in gray VMI uniforms.

Unclaimed rifles are gathered and stacked on the ground, while discarded leather equipment, cartridge pouches, hats, belts, and other accouterments are gathered in piles for later sorting.

With failing hope, Moses still wanders, searching for his missing friends. He spots a cart with a wounded soldier in it, then notices the cart pass a cadet lying facedown in the mud. His heart jumps. He rushes over to the cadet on the ground.

"Garland?"

Garland Jefferson's curly blond hair is dirty and matted. His right hand, mangled and bloodied, still clasps the barrel of his rifle in a death grip. With extreme effort, Moses pulls on Garland's clothes to turn him over. He is horrified to see that the left shoulder and chest of Garland's jacket is soaked with black blood and caked with dirt. Having found him, he grows desperate, unsure if his friend is alive or dead.

"Garland, come on," Moses pleads.

He feels Garland move slightly and is infused with a glimmer of hope. He pulls on his friend, panting, "Hey, yah. Hey, yah," and struggles to lift him up. Moses waves to the cart being pulled up the hill by cadets. "You! Come over here! You got a stretcher?"

The cadets bring over a stretcher, and Moses helps roll Garland over and onto it. A few women and medical workers help Moses lift the stretcher onto the open bed of the cart. They struggle with the inert weight of the litter and its burden to shove it on without disturbing the silent cadet who already occupies one side of the wagon and lies very still. Moses grunts with each exertion but keeps reassuring Garland, whether he can hear or not, "It'll be alright. It'll be alright. It'll.…"

In a corner of the scattered remains of the struggle for the hill, Sam thinks he recognizes the shape of a body lying face down in the mud. Hobbling over, his hopes rise. Shedding his canteen, Sam drops his rifle crutch and falls onto the ground next to John, who lies still unconscious and undisturbed. Sam only sees that he lies very still. He rolls John over and presses his ear to his chest. He's not sure. Sam then puts three fingers to John's throat to feel for a pulse.

He's alive! "There you go, Johnny! Can you hear me?"

The movement has served to bring John around a bit. His eyes flutter. Weak and confused, he is unable to focus or even to speak, but he begins to blink as from a long dream. He looks up and is greeted by Sam's beaming grin.

"There you go! There you go! John! Can you hear me?" Sam's relief at finding his friend alive spreads through them both. He gently turns his friend's head to face straight up. John's features are cut, bloody, and smeared with mud. But he is alive.

Sam openly laughs as John finally regains enough awareness to keep his eyes open and to look around speculatively, still confused. "There you go, Johnny. Can you hear me? Johnny?" Sam clutches John's hand firmly and shares the news. "Johnny, we won the battle. All of us."

John struggles to move his head to the left, then back to the right as he tries to take in the scene around them.

Still breathless, Sam continues, "People gonna call us heroes now."

John sees the body of a nearby cadet lying face up in the mud, courses of dried blood from the corner of his mouth and sightless eyes staring skyward. Painfully rousing himself, John works to gather his thoughts. Still blinking in the hesitancy of renewed consciousness, he tries to speak. The words come slowly, freighted with deep sorrow.

"They're the heroes."

Sam takes this in and looks out over the destruction of so many men, the drifting smoke, and the small figures moving within the huge landscape below. He comes to see what John knows, his thoughts complete when John adds, "Jack...." He takes a breath, and then finishes, "All of them."

All the day's trials, anxiety, triumph, and loss, the excruciating finality of what has happened, along with the suppurating wound in his leg congeal for Sam in the quiet insight of John's words. At long last he surrenders the last of the strength that has kept him going until this moment. He lets his head drop softly onto John's chest as the alchemy of unprecedented exhaustion and overwhelming grief finally overcome him. His reserves gone, he is spent.

Bring Them Inside

On the busy lawn of the Clinedinst estate, now serving as a field hospital, slender sunbeams slant through the trees leaving bright petals of light on the grass. The grounds are crowded with wounded and dying young men, while women and a few doctors hurry among them doing all they can under the pressure of time.

A young cadet sits on the ground with a fixed stare in his eyes. His hand holds a piece of straw and twitches uncontrollably.

A woman, too young to have to perform such duty, carefully presses a cloth onto a still-bleeding wound. Another gives a wounded soldier a stiff drink of whisky to numb the pain.

Mrs. Clinedinst hurries out of the house carrying a tray with more bandages. Pouring onto the lawn through the front gateway is an alarming procession of wounded soldiers, some hobbling on sticks, some carried, some being supported by their companions, and nearly all filthy and in clothes stained with blood.

She indicates a group of the wounded and orders, "Bring them inside!" and turns back to the house. On her way, she passes a young girl whose bloodied hands press a red-stained rag onto the face of a young soldier with a terrible head wound. To each side lie those for whom the attention of the ladies is too late. Laid out on their backs and on their sides, some with eyes closed, they are terribly still, the congealed blood on their faces and on their clothes no longer fresh.

Inside the residence, Mrs. Clinedinst hurries through a room to bring supplies to one of the older girls tending a soldier who cries in pain as he tries to lift himself onto a table.

Using only the light of a high window, a surgeon saws at the leg of a soldier. Helpers struggle to hold down the screaming patient.

Mrs. Clinedinst comes through the main room with its yawning fireplace, where flames are tended to keep scraps of cloth boiling. She passes through a band of shadow and comes back to the front door just as its outside light is blocked by three figures. The one in the middle is a new patient. He is supported by Duck and Moses. It is Sam Atwill. He is gray from loss of blood and no longer has the strength to hold himself up.

Mrs. Clinedinst looks down and is shaken by the sight of Sam's wound. His right trouser leg is soaked and black with a slurry of bloody mud, and she can barely make out his bare foot, a useless dangling appendage, russet brown and caked with earth that the bleeding has kept wet. "Look at that wound!" she gasps, barely concealing her shock.

Mrs. Clinedinst quickly orders, "Take this young man into the back bedroom!"

Sam recognizes Libby's mother. He woozily pleads, "Could I speak with Libby? Just for a minute."

"Oh, son, Lib's not here," she tells him. "She's in the field with the older girls."

A young girl in the next room overhears the exchange—the same girl who had asked Sam for a dance at the party before the battle. She recognizes Sam's voice and enters the room apprehensively. She looks on as Duck and Moses carry Sam toward the back room, trailing Sam's dirty blood along the floor.

That Boy

The last of the smoke wafts thinly away from the now-quiet battlefield. A bird chirps on the evening air. Equipment, shoes, rifles, and bodies still litter the ground. At the bottom of the hard-fought Bushong's Hill and trailing up the darkened face, are scores of lost shoes mired in the wet and trampled earth.

Weary litter bearers continue their task, carrying away the wounded on stretchers. A lone wagon makes its way along the access road. Old Judge, his deeply lined face hanging like worn leather from a peg, sits disconsolately at the reins, immersed in grief. He has witnessed many classes come and go through the Institute, but none quite like this one. Now, like Charon, boatman of the underworld, he slowly transports the broken remains of his charges, the creak of the wheels sharp on the quiet air.

On the field, a girl with dark hair pulled back with a blue ribbon that matches the color of her incongruously tasteful dress tends to a wounded Confederate soldier. Libby is dirty, her once-lovely dress stained with the blood of many men. Yet she remains in the midst of this unprecedented agony to make herself more useful than ever before.

From across the field, the girl who watched them bring Sam into the house runs urgently, calling and stumbling through the grass in her house shoes. Libby stands as the girl nears.

The anxious girl takes Libby by the arms and gasps breathlessly, "He's at the house! That boy. He's wounded, but he's asking for you!"

Libby hugs the girl in gratitude, and with genuine excitement all but yells, "Thank you so much!" She hands the bandages to girl and hurries away through the grass.

The girl takes Libby's place and begins to attend the wounded man on the ground.

All My Sons

At the Clinedinst residence, Garland lies on a table, rolled onto his left side. His shirt has been cut away, and the front of his right shoulder is wrapped with a bandage now nearly soaked through with dark blood. He is only semiconscious. An older doctor stands behind him and works to pull the bullet out of his back while Moses sits anxiously in front of the table on a short stool, holding Garland's hand in both of his.

The doctor is tired. His long sleeves are quite stained with the gore of his duties, and though his vest is open, he maintains the dignity of his office with his bow tie in place. He is drawn and exhausted, but there is too much to do. He must not stop.

Mrs. Clinedinst approaches and stands next to the doctor.

"Will he … survive?" she asks quietly.

The doctor holds up a bloody forceps clasping a metal rifle ball and says evenly, "The bullet went through his chest and lodged in his back."

He drops the bullet into a metal bowl. The slug makes an ugly clank as it strikes and tumbles in the bowl.

Mrs. Clinedinst looks back down at Garland, at the large red stain covering the bandage. Her face twists with heartache and anguish.

Observing Mrs. Clinedinst's deep concern, the doctor turns to her and asks thoughtfully, "Is this your son?"

Mrs. Clinedinst looks across the room. She takes a breath as tears fill her eyes. She opens her hands, motioning to the entire house, filled with wounded soldiers. "These are all my sons," she says.

Emotion overcomes her, and she looks away, walking slowly from the room as the doctor and his only nurse return their focus to the urgent needs at hand.

Moses looks up. He releases Garland's hand and quickly stands up from the stool. He hurries to catch Mrs. Clinedinst before she leaves the room.

"Ma'am?" he says haltingly.

Mrs. Clinedinst pauses and turns around. Respectfully, Moses removes his hat as he draws closer.

His eyes are swollen and red. His face is marred with dirt, and his hair is matted against his head. "Do you have a New Testament?" he asks, his voice soft as if trying not to disturb her.

Mrs. Clinedinst shows a hint of surprise at the request. She turns, opens a drawer, and pulls out a Bible.

She turns back and hands the Bible to Moses. Unsure if this is what he really wants, she ventures, "This is a Christian Bible. I understand that you're … Jewish?"

Moses is not surprised by the question. "I am a Jew. It's for my friend. I do not believe God would object."

Mrs. Clinedinst's face softens, and reverently Moses takes the Bible from her hands and nods.

"Thank you," he says and goes directly back to the table, where the doctor and the nurse wrap Garland's shoulder. Moses sits down next to his friend, Bible in hand.

Mrs. Clinedinst looks back at the two boys with affection, as proud as any mother could be of her sons.

As the evening comes on, the sun emerges through a layer of cloud and bathes the suffering in the yard with a warm yellow light. Women scurry among the wounded, doing what they can to comfort the boys and men who lie in the grass under the trees.

Sam's wound has been tended, but he has lost too much blood and is carried outside and placed on the crowded front lawn to make room for others inside and to be given some fresh air. His jacket is off, revealing Libby's blue ribbon tied to one of the straps of his suspenders. He fingers the ribbon tenderly as he searches the ladies in attendance, hoping still to see his Libby. Yet all around seems chaos and confusion and moans of pain while still more wounded are flowing in. Nearby, a very young girl struggles with a bucket of water, doing what she can to help.

Sam looks around desperately. His mouth opens as he labors to breathe. He runs his fingers down the blue satin ribbon, his only comfort in the pain that spreads though him. He tries to brace himself up against a tree, and with blurring eyesight, he scans the yard. He is a man fast becoming lost, and there is suddenly something desperate in his efforts. Then, overcome with exhaustion, he loses his struggle and falls face down onto the grass of the front yard. He lands with a groan.

One of the young ladies in attendance comes down to his side to help and asks, "Are you alright?"

The young woman lifts up Sam's right arm. Sam's face turns as he lifts slightly out of the grass. Blinking, he fights to stay conscious as he looks down to his leg.

Blood now streams freely from his reopened bayonet wound, flowing through the bandage and onto the grass. His breathing becomes labored. He cannot afford the blood loss, and his eyes tell her that all he had ever wanted to be is draining away.

Through the fog, he struggles to focus, to conjure up his most precious memories: his first glimpse of Libby's face at the door of the girls' community house, the vision of Libby hurrying down the stairs that last night to say goodbye before the march to battle, the softness of her hands cupping his face, the warmth of her arms around his neck, the tenderness of her lips, and their spoken and unspoken promises of a lifetime filled with love, laughter, and conversation.

Sam drifts through these memories, his mind reaching to grasp them, to hold on to them forever. He sees Libby's face bathed in the soft glow of evening light at the dance and remembers her teasing him just before her kiss. She had loved him back, and that final thought gives him peace.

Light Me a Candle

With darkness descending outside, isolating the suffering from view and making the groans of pain somehow louder, the inside of the Clinedinst home grows dim, and a few candles appear.

Garland Jefferson lies on a bed in front of the fireplace, semiconscious. His head rests on a pillow. A blanket covers his chest to keep off the blood-loss chills. Moses still sits loyally nearby and holds the Bible open. A lone candle flickers faintly on the mantle providing barely enough light for Moses to read, softly, "From the fourteenth chapter of Saint John. 'Let not your heart be troubled. Ye believe in God, believe also in me.'"

Mrs. Clinedinst comes in and places another candle on the mantle. Moses continues reading, "In my Father's house there are many mansions. If it were not so…" Overcome, he stops, choking back the tears.

Mrs. Clinedinst places her hand on Garland's shoulder, and Moses digs deep within himself. For the sake of his dear friend, he finds the strength to continue with the verse, "…I would have told you."

Without a word, Mrs. Clinedinst leaves as Moses goes on. "I go to prepare a place for you."

In a gravelly, weak whisper, Garland interrupts. His eyes are fixed as he asks Moses, "Would you … would you light me a candle? I don't want to listen in the dark."

Moses stops. He looks down at his friend, then over to candles already throwing light out from the nearby fireplace mantle. The end is near.

Moses tries again to speak, but is choked with emotion. He cannot go on. In silent despair, he rests his hand on Garland's head and strokes his friend's hair. Then he drops his head onto the pillow next to Garland's. He inches near enough to place his forehead gently against his dying friend's head, and his eyes fill with tears as he girds himself for the final goodbye to the friend he loved as a brother.

That Godforsaken Valley

In the darkness of night, General Grant sits at a table outside his command tent, reading and smoking a cigar by lamplight. In the background, a silver river moves slowly in the glow of moonlight.

Strewn on the table before him are rolled maps; nearby, a whisky glass.

An aide strides forward and delivers a paper. Grant takes it and, holding it at arm's length, squints to read. Not good news. Grant manages an understated reaction. "My, my, my." Disgusted, he throws the paper down onto the table.

"Find me a man who knows how to set a fire next time we go into that godforsaken valley."

He looks grimly into the night sky.

"We burn it to cinders."

News of Defeat

President Abraham Lincoln stands stiffly, reading official papers as his military aides wait nearby.

A uniformed aide steps up and hands the president a piece of folded paper. Lincoln takes the paper. The aide motions everyone toward the door. "Let's leave him, gentlemen."

Alone, the president reads the dispatch in silence. As the large doors slowly close, the president is left, as so often before, alone with the ponderous weight of the nation's fate on his shoulders. His tired face tightens at the bad news. He finishes reading, and his hands drop wearily to his sides.

The Dream That Died

At the Clinedinst residence, Libby walks slowly into a room. In front of her a body lies on an elevated table, a white sheet covering the head. Libby's mother follows closely behind her.

Libby does not cry. She gently pulls back the sheet to see for herself. Sam's handsome face, still smudged with dirt, is unfamiliarly pale. She stares for a long moment then reaches across Sam's chest and touches the blue ribbon still attached to his suspender strap. She leans down and places a light and tender kiss on his cold lips.

She cannot tear her eyes from the face of the young man she knew for such a short time and yet loved so deeply. She straightens up as she continues to run her fingers over the blue satin ribbon. *Tonight* he had said, his voice a mere whisper, *I believe in love at first sight.* And so had she.

Unaware of the depth of her daughter's feelings, Libby's mother watches her daughter struggle to keep her emotions in check. And then, as the harsh reality begins to sink in, Libby's eyes fill with tears. This is truly the end of her dream, their dream. At last she whispers a singular lament, "We were going to spend our lives. Together."

Sam's absence fills the room as Libby's tears spill down the curve of her cheeks. She lingers a moment longer for a last look at the man she loved and in whom she had invested such hope. As she turns slowly to her mother, Mrs. Clinedinst draws Libby in close to her heart. Resting her confused, weary head on her mother's chest, Libby begins to sob.

Mrs. Clinedinst puts a gentle hand on her daughter's head and looks down in her own silent goodbye to Cadet Sam Atwill and the dreams that died with him.

No Thought At All

In the front room of the shell-damaged Bushong farmhouse, the furniture has been hastily moved aside to convert the space into a field hospital. John lies on the floor along with a few others. He is partially covered with a child's blanket, and his shirt has been removed to reveal a deep gash in his left shoulder. An attempt has been made to clean the wound, but otherwise it remains unattended. He wears bandages on smaller injuries, and his face is smudged despite a hasty attempt to clean him up. Behind him on his own section of hard plank flooring lies his friend, Duck. Both are surrounded by other patients and attendants.

General Breckinridge and Major Semple step into the room, respectfully removing their hats. John attempts to rise up on his elbow as the general approaches.

Breckinridge greets the young men. "Mr. Wise. Mr. Colonna." The young men are surprised but cautious, uncertain of why their ranking commanders are paying them a visit.

Breckinridge begins. "I am told you cadets decided to lead the charge on your own volition." Allowing it to sink in, he asks, "Is that so?"

John looks up. Duck remains at supine attention, silent.

The general continues sternly, challenging them. "Are they not teaching you the value of the chain of command at the Institute?"

John answers, admonished, and deeply exhausted, "I am sorry, sir."

"Are you?" Breckinridge says. "Hmm," he says as he pauses to underscore his admonition. "And what in good God's name were you thinking?"

John's reddened eyes and drawn face betray that this is a last straw to the worst day of his life. His body, scarred, crudely bandaged, all energy depleted, sags. He turns his war-worn face beseechingly up to the general.

"My father says the best thing about doing what's right is that it requires no thought …" John drops his weary head. "… no thought at all."

Drawing in a deep breath, Breckinridge answers, pride and admiration in his voice. "Well, guess I have to thank you … for not thinking."

The general smiles broadly, and John, his eyes filling with tears, manages a weak smile in return. Duck holds himself stiffly at attention, still not sure. But Breckinridge reaches out his hand and Duck clasps it.

"Well done, Virginians," Breckinridge says. "Well done, men."

"Thank you, sir," John says.

And then General Breckinridge turns to leave, followed, as usual, by Major Semple.

The Battle is Done

A cadet staff officer wanders through the littered landscape, searching the ground for something, perhaps for someone. Old Judge is still at work trying to account for any of his charges who may have been overlooked during the earlier collection efforts. He pushes a cart through the mud, pausing from time to time to examine another forlorn gray heap on the ground.

Nearby, a dazed and confused Sir Rat stumbles around the silent bog at the base of the hard-fought hill, holding several shoes in his arms. His face is smeared with mud, his eyes red. He has found his hat, which is crumpled and dirty but is perched on his head in a dutiful facsimile of regulation wear. He collapses on the ground next to another body.

Old Judge pauses in his search and scans the battlefield. No stranger to conflict and cruelty, he surveys the carnage, shaking his head wearily at the folly of man. He looks down to find a lone cadet's boot stuck in the mud.

Nearby, young Sir Rat pulls another lost shoe from the muck and carefully wipes the mud from the leather upper and sole. Seated in the mud with his collection of shoes, he reverentially places the new one next to the others.

Old Judge approaches the boy carefully and kneels to put his arms around his small shoulders. He pulls the youngster close, and as Sir Rat looks up into the familiar face, he finally breaks, burying his face in Old Judge's chest, letting the tears flow and at last surrendering to the enormity of the world. He weeps for the crushing loss of so many friends, the first strangers he had ever met, friends who had taken him in, had mentored him, and who had made him part of a family. Things would never be the same for him ever again—indeed, they would never be the same for anyone. Ever.

Sir Rat has done a man's work this day, but Old Judge knows he is still a boy and needs a boy's comfort. He wraps his large hand around the boy's head and holds him close. Alone in the shattered landscape, the old man and the young boy, remnants of outrage, cling together in the mud, rocking slowly as the shadows close around them.

Old Judge knows the sun sets on the living and the dead, but as the vast cloak of evening settles over the battlefield, sanctifying the horrors of the day beneath a shroud of starlight, the living must go on living.

A Tribute in Film

Epilogue

We have attempted to tell the story of a few of the brave sons of Virginia who died at New Market. In the final scenes of the film, the sun shines on the three well-tended graves at the foot of the Woman Who Mourns on the VMI grounds. A small flag of Virginia marks each stone. The polished green marble tablets, set into red brick, are etched with names.

Cadet Jacqueline B. Stanard. Private, Company B Corps of Cadets

Jack, who had flashed his smile that day in Chinook's office at Sir Rat's definition of the meaning of honor.

Cadet Thomas G. Jefferson. Private, Company B, Corps of Cadets

Garland, the aristocratic Virginian who had danced with such delight the night before the last day's march, had died with his dear friend Moses sitting with him until he drew his final breath.

Cadet Samuel F. Atwill. Corporal, Company A Corps of Cadets

Sam, who had not believed in anything dear enough to fight for until the moment he saw Libby, had loved his friends so well he allowed himself to bleed to death rather than give up the search for survivors.

To this day, the legacy of these three friends and all the other VMI cadets who fought and died at New Market is formally commemorated at VMI by the entire Corps of Cadets, assembled on the parade ground in full dress uniforms.

A ceremonial roll call begins as the cadets account for those of their brothers in arms lost in battle and who cannot respond for themselves.

A cadet steps forward and lifts his rifle smartly to "present arms," his weapon held squarely in front of his face. He calls out, "Private Stanard, died on the field of honor, sir!"

A second cadet steps forward, in turn, and sounds off, "Private Jefferson, died on the field of honor, sir!"

A third cadet, an African-American, makes his report, "Corporal Atwill, died on the field of honor, sir!"

The film, *Field of Lost Shoes*, focused on a particular group of friends whom we came to know as we retraced their story. But there were others who died that day, and they will not be forgotten, either. They, too, are remembered as the roll call ceremony continues.

The senior cadet officer present brings his sword, then lowers the blade and holds it at the salute position. He reports to the superintendent and to the commandant the remaining names of cadets lost at New Market. "Private Crockett, Private Hartsfield, Private Haynes...." The list goes on.

The superintendent, a general in the United States Army, and the commandant, a colonel of artillery, stand at attention in dress blue uniforms and hold their salutes.

In the closing scene of the movie, cadets stand at the gravesite in sad repose and mourning. The flag of Virginia fills the screen against a background of silver-lined clouds. The senior cadet's roll call continues, "…Private Jones, Private McDowell, Private Wheelwright, Sergeant Cabell, died on the field of honor, sir!"

But the VMI ceremony does more than honor these cadets. It honors all the souls lost to the Civil War. And there are more stories to tell, more lives changed forever by the Battle of New Market and the war itself.

There is Old Judge baking bread and beckoning his cadets to come eat. Old Judge became a free man and continued running the bakery at VMI until he retired after thirty years of service.

And there is Moses, smiling endearingly, sketching with charcoal that afternoon by the pond before the dance. Moses Ezekiel, the first Jewish cadet to attend VMI, became an internationally famous sculptor. He work is installed around the world, and he is buried in the shadow of his massive sculpture commemorating the Civil War at Arlington National Cemetery. Among his works is Virginia Mourning Her Dead, the statue standing over the graves of the cadets—his schoolmates and friends—who died at New Market.

There is Duck Colonna on top of the hill, his pistol raised above his head in triumph at the battle's end. Duck eventually rebuilt his family home, became a school teacher, and entered a long career in U.S. government service.

We remember young Robert, Sir Rat, raising his rifle into the air on top of the hill, on top of the field of lost shoes. To this day, VMI cadets, both male and female, refer to their classmates as "Brother Rat."

And we remember John Wise and how he relaxed in his barracks room, book in hand, enjoying the camaraderie of friends just before Sir Rat brought the news of Old Judge's beating. John served in the United States Congress and helped to rebuild the Union.

And we will always remember the slaves and the dehumanizing brutality they suffered at slave auctions similar to the one Governor Wise sent young John into to decide for himself what was right and what was wrong. That auction house, known as Lumpkin's Jail, was eventually bought by former slave Mary Lumpkin and converted into a school for free slaves. From that humble beginning, the Virginia Union University was born.

Finally, the film takes one final look through the vaulting stained glass windows at the front of the VMI chapel, through which large Virginia and American flags fill the screen, slowly unfurling in a gentle breeze.

Following the war, the Virginia Military Institute resumed its appointed mission of educating leaders for Virginia and the nation.

Acknowledgements

A memorial entitled "in grateful memory" lists individuals who inspired the making of the film:

Joan and Peter Farrell
Honorable Elmon T. Gray
Robert H. Patterson, Jr.
Marjorie Fowler Jenkins
Joseph Stephen Kennedy
John Crisp Coleman
Robert Williamson
Robert Ridley Hagan

Credits, Cast and Crew

a
TREDEGAR FILMWORKS
production

in association with
BROOKWELL McNAMARA
ENTERTAINMENT

a
SEAN McNAMARA
film
FIELD OF LOST SHOES
BASED ON A TRUE STORY

DAVID ARQUETTE
LUKE BENWARD
MAX LLOYD-JONES
ZACH ROERIG

JOSH ZUCKERMAN
KEITH DAVID
LAUREN HOLLY
MARY MOUSER
NOLAN GOULD
SEAN MARQUETTE
PARKER CROFT
GALE HAROLD
COURTNEY GAINS
WERNER DAEHN
JOHN RIXEY MOORE
MICHAEL GOODWIN
with
JASON ISAACS
and
TOM SKERRITT

&

casting by
Joey Paul Jensen, CSA
costume designer
KEVIN R. HERSHBERGER
music composed by
FREDERIK WIEDMANN
production design
DAWN R. FERRY
edited by
JEFF W. CANAVAN
director of photography
BRAD SHIELD, ACS
line producer
ELIZABETH RIDLEY HAGAN

co-producers
JEFF CANAVAN
PETER FARRELL
JOEY PAUL JENSON
KEVIN R. HERSHBERGER
co-executive producers
ALAN PAO
SEAN McNAMARA
TREVOR DRINKWATER

&

executive producer
BRANDON K. HOGAN
produced by
THOMAS F. FARRELL II
DAVID M. KENNEDY
story by
THOMAS F. FARRELL II
&
DAVID M. KENNEDY
screenplay by
DAVID M. KENNEDY
&
THOMAS F. FARRELL II
and
RON BASS
directed by
SEAN McNAMARA

Unit Production Manager - JULIE BUCK
First Assistant Director - YANN SOBEZYNSKI
Second Assistant Director - BARBARA LONTKOWSKI

Cast

Abraham Lincoln	MICHAEL KREBS
Armisted	JAKE LAWSON
Benjamin "Duck" Colonna	SEAN MARQUETTE
Captain Henry A. DuPont	DAVID ARQUETTE
Captain Chinook	COURTNEY GAINS
Confederate Soldier #1	STEVE LEBENS
Confederate Soldier #2	COBY BATTY
Doctor	WILLIAM FLAMAN
DuPont Aide de Camp	DUTCH HOFSTETTER
Garland Jefferson	PARKER CROFT
General Breckinridge	JASON ISAACS
General Franz Sigel	WERNER DAEHN
General Ulysses S. Grant	TOM SKERRITT
General Wharton	JOE INSCOE
Girl from the Dance	ALEXA YEAMES
Girl Trapped Under Wagon	TIFFANY FLOURNOY
Governor Wise	JOHN RIXEY MOORE
Hawker	ERIK AUDE
Israel	GOGO LOMO-DAVID
Jack Stanard	ZACH ROERIG
John Wise	LUKE BENWARD
Libby Clinedinst	MARY MOUSER
Lincoln Advisor	THOMAS FARRELL
Major Charles Semple	GALE HAROLD
Martha Ann	BRANDI NICOLE FEEMSTER
Moses Ezekiel	JOSH ZUCKERMAN
Mrs. Clinedinst	LAUREN HOLLY
Old Judge	KEITH DAVID
Old Spex	FRANK AARD
Robert / Sir Rat	NOLAN GOULD
Sam Atwill	MAX LLOYD-JONES

Secretary of State Seward	MICHAEL GOODWIN
Sentry	ALEXANDER SPENCE WINTER
Slave Girl	SHADAYAH MAE
Soldier	FLOYD HENDERSON
Union Infantry Officer	PETER FARRELL
Union Soldier #1	SEAN PATRICK MCNAMARA
Union Soldier #2	DAVID KENNEDY
Young John Wise	SEAN RYAN FOX
Young VMI Cadet #1	JETT HOGAN
Young VMI Cadet #2	MARK McNAMARA

Featured Virginia Military Institute Cadets

SPENCER S. ALLEN
CHRISTIAN P. BEALE
RYAN M. DICK
ANDREW E. EPPS
MICHAEL R. KIRKPATRICK
J. TAYLOR MONFORT-EATON
CONNOR P. MORGAN
NATHAN C. MYERS
RILEY H. NEWSOM
SEAN P. NOLL
KEVIN C. PONSLER
XAVIER T. SCOTT
ABHIMANYU TRIKHA
DARREN M. WATERS
CHRISTOPHER M. WISNOWSKI
JACOB ZENT

Stunt Players	JEFF GUMS
	STEVE GUMS

JASON GUPTON
CHAD HESSLER
IAN HURDLE
ERIC MIRANDA
KID RICHMOND
ROSS MORGAN RUBEN
NICK STANNER
JOSH TESSIER

Associate Producers	RICK MORGAN
	BOB PARSLEY
	RON BASS
Production Supervisor	MERRY DUNNING
B Camera Operator/Steadicam	MICHAEL P. MAY
A Camera First Assistant	TONY RIVETTI, SR.
A Camera Second Assistant	ROD SANDOVAL
A Camera Additional Second Assistants	BRANDON PONTICELLE
	SEAN SUTPHIN
B Camera First Assistant	BRETT PETERS
B Camera Second Assistant	JAY HAGER
Digital Imaging Technician	EDUARDO EGUIA
Additional Assistant Camera	PATRICK MOYNAHAN
Camera Loaders	SON DOUNG
	LEW FRAGA
Art Director	JEREMIAH HORNBAKER
Set Decorator	ERIC HUNSAKER
Leadman	STEVE SHIFFLETTE
On-Set Dresser	JAMIE BISHOP
Property Master	STEVEN H. GEORGE

Assistant Property Master	JOHN D. BERT
Cannon Master	BOB GILLMOR
Armorer	J. RYAN SMITH
Property PA	JACOB COPPAGE
Additional Prop Assistant	CYNTHIA GIRON
Swing	RYAN JOHANSEN
	GRESHAM POLLARD
	KEVIN QUICK
Swing/Greens	GRESHAM POLLARD
Construction Coordinator	JAMES THOMPSON
Scenic	CHRISTIAN QUICK
Special Effects Coordinator	BRIAN MERRICK
Special Effects Foreman	AUSTIN MURRAY
Special Effects Assistants	SHAWN HAMBRIGHT
	DAN NELSON
	JIM SCHRUEFER
Costume Supervisor	AMBER GIVENS
Set Costumers	CARL I. JOHNSON
	AMANDA POWELL
Women's Costumer	JULIANNE HERCZEG
Assistant Women's Dresser	MARY CHALLMAN
Costume Assistants	ALYSSA FORD
	VANESSA BUCK
Stitchers	CHRISTI OWEN
	HEATHER BISCHOFF
	SHELBY DAY
	KRISHNA KINGSLAY
	CHARLES WISSINGER
Sound Mixer	ANDREW UVAROV
Boom Operator	STEVE SAADA
Utility Sound	PROCTOR TRIVETTE

Gaffer	JIM GILSON
Best Boy Electric	JOE MARTENS
Rigging Gaffer	JOHN MARTENS
Electricians	TOBY LeCHEMINANT
	CHASE LIVENGOOD
	ROBERT LOPEZ
	JOHN McGONEGLE
	JUAN MENDOZA
Key Grip	MARK EVANS
Best Boy Grip	JAMES DOMBEY
Dolly Grip	VERNON WYNN
Company Grips	DAVID BARRY
	GORDON MARTIN
	IAN MONTROSS
Additional Grips	TIM BROWNE III
	SCOTT DUVALL
	JASON HALL
	GARY KING
Script Supervisor	LISA WHITTINGTON
Second Second Assistant Director	CASEY MAKO
Set Production Assistants	SARAH L. CHURCH
	JENNIFER ELLIS
	MARLEY GOETZ
	AVERY KENNEDY
	CHRIS RICHARDSON
	TOM SANCHEZ PRUNIER
Additional Set PAs	YASAMAN AGHAEINEJAD
	DANIEL BAGBEY
	NATE FLEMING
	CALEB JACKSON

	SAM KENNEDY
	WALKER STETTINIUS
Still Photographer	TONY RIVETTI, JR.
Storyboard Artist	LEN MORGANTI
Production Coordinator	LIZA TULLIDGE
Assistant Production Coordinator	VINCENT FARRELL
Office Production Assistants	DIANE GUNTER
	BEN WURST
Additional Office PAs	BRANT TULLIDGE
	JAMES NAUGHTON
Production Intern	REEF HOGAN
Location Manager	LAURA BRYANT
Assistant Location Manager	PEG CROWDER
Locations PA's	MARLEY GOETZ
	COLTON SULLIVAN
	MATT TAYLOR
Production Accountant	ELIZABETH RIDLEY HAGAN
Payroll Accountant	SHAYNE BLAKEY
Accounting Assistant	CHANDRA TOURTELOT
Accounting Clerk	FRANCES COKE DOBBINS
Makeup Department Head	JOE HURT
Key Makeup Artist	BRYAN REYNOLDS
Makeup Artists	SHELLY ILLMENSEE
	JENNIFER McCOLLOM
	HEATHER TOLER
Hair Department Head	KARYN ALEXANDER HUSTON
Key Hairstylist	LYNETTE RIMMER
Hairstylist	SHIRLEY S. BAKER

Casting Consultant	NINER PARIKH
Associate Casting	KIMBERLY BENNINK
Location Casting	HENRY JADERLUND
	DR. SHERI BIAS
Reenactor Coordinator	GUY WILLIAM GANE III
Background Casting Assistant	ALICIA AYOUB
Casting Intern	EMILY KASP
Assistant to Mr. Kennedy and Mr. Farrell	GARLAND PARSLEY
Assistant to Mr. McNamara	ROB CAVEDO
Assistant to Mr. Hogan	BAILEY ENOCHS
Transportation Coordinator	KRIS GOLASHESKY
Transportation Captain	ROBERT FOSTER, SR.
Drivers	DENNIS ADAMS
	BILL BENNER
	PHILLIP CREWS
	GERALD DANIEL
	ROBBIE DOWDY
	BRIAN ELLIS
	JAMES GARRETT
	B.J. HALLETT
	JO HARRIS
	BOBBY JONES
	LARRY JONES
	STEVEN CONWAY LOVING
	ALBERT MITCHELL
	ROBERT O'CONNELL
	PATRICIA PICKENS
	ELLIS PRYOR
	WALTER WHEELHOUSE
Catering provided by	GROOVIN' GOURMETS

Craft Services	BLACKDOG CATERING THERESA & STEVE CRAIG
Medical Services provided by	SET SAFETY RICHMOND JUSTIN DALE BENNETT
Animals Head Wrangler	DOUG SLOAN
Additional Wrangler	LUKE CONNER
From Go Pro	PAUL CRANDELL JUSTIN WILKENFELD

SECOND UNIT

Second Unit Director	THOMAS WHELAN
Director of Photography	ERIC HURT
First Assistant Director	SCOTT CARTER
First Assistant Camera	TIM RISCH
Second Assistant Camera	DANY CAPORALETTI CALEB PLUTZER
Gaffer	JASON MITCHELL
Aerial Scout Unit	QUINTON WEISKITTEL

POST PRODUCTION

Assistant Editor	BILL YOUNG
Supervising Sound Editor	CHRISTIAN DWIGGINS
Sound Designer	CHRIS TRENT
Dialogue Editor	GARRAD WHATLEY
Sound Editor	LAUREN ROBINSON
Re-Recording Mixer	CHRISTIAN DWIGGINS
Legal By	CHRISTY DURAN
Credit and Stock License Administrator	ASHLEY HASZ
Post Production Assistant	JOSH STEIN

Digital Dailies by	TUNNEL POST
	Santa Monica, California
Dailies Editors	TAYLOR MAHONY
	JORDAN DODGE
	MOMO YU-WEN HSIAO
Data Manager	JOHN BERRY
Post Production Facilities Provided by	TUNNEL POST
	Santa Monica, California
Tunnel Post Post Production Assistant	ELLEXA LEMARIE
Tunnel Post Post Production PA	CAROLINE JONES
Digital Intermediate Services Provided By	TUNNEL POST
	Santa Monica, California
DI Producers	ALAN PAO
	HEATHER TOLL
DI Colorist	SEBASTIAN PEREZ-BURCHARD
Digital Conform	TAYLOR MAHONY
	J.D. MOORE
End Titles	SATSUKI MAY ASAI
VFX Producer / VFX Supervisor	MITCH SUSKIN
VFX Coordinator	JAMES FUJISAKI
Digital Artist	ROBERT SHORT
Roto Artist	KAREN BAKKE

HIMANI PRODUCTIONS

Compositing Supervisor	KEVIN KUTCHAVER
Composite Artists	STEPHEN MITCHELL
	PHIL CARBONARO
	ERIC REINHARD

BLACKPOOL STUDIOS
Matte Artist   ERIC CHAUVIN

SEVEN CROWS VFX
Composite Artists   STEVE FONG
                                                DAVY NETHERCUTT

BRAZEN PICTURES
Digital Supervisor   MARK KOCHINSKI
Digital Artists   KEVIN KIPPER
                                                IAN MACKEY
Modeler   PIERRE DROLET

CRC PUBLIC RELATIONS
                                    MARIA HATZIKONSTANTINOU
                                    MICHAEL W. THOMPSON, JR.
                                                KEITH APPELL
                                                HUGH K. NORTON
                                                JESSIE T. MARKELL
                                                CARLY O'LOUGHLIN

Public Relations Consultant   EVA T. HARDY

Orchestration   HYESU YANG
Original Score conducted by   HYESU YANG
                                                DZIJAN EMIN
Original Score produced by   FREDERIK WIEDMANN
Music Preparation   DAVID BERTOK
Assistant to Composer   DAVID BERTOK
Original Score performed by   F.A.M.E.'S. PROJECT
                                    MACEDONIAN RADIO SYMPHONIC
                                                ORCHESTRA
                                                SKOPJE, MACEDONIA

Sound Engineer	GEORGII HRISTOVSKI
Protools Engineer	BOBAN APOSTOLOV
Stage Managers	RISTE TRAJKOVSKI
	EVTIM RISTOV
Solo Trumpet	CHRIS TEDESCO
Additional Music Contracting	CHRIS TEDESCO

John Barleycorn & Me
Music by Frederik Wiedmann (BMI)
Lyrics by Harold Payne (BMI)
Performed by Harold Payne
Published by Harold Payne Music (BMI) and Feda Music (BMI)

Credited Background Actors
Aaron Forum, Addison Hagan, Adrian Nanney, Al Underwood,
Amos Richardson, Andrew Mayfield, Andrew Trongone,
David Elliott, Deborah Vincent, Dot Gregory,
Gordy Price, Hunter Maddox, Isabella Johnson, Jacob Brankley,
Jay Butler, Justin Bias, Justin Gardner, Kaitlin Jones,
Keely Thompson, Kevin Criner, Kyle Cryer, Leah McNamara,
Mason Campbell, Meghan Mayfield, Nick Costa, Ryan Jacques,
Steven Correal, Tanner Bluewolf, Tucker Conley

Historical Background Provided by
THE BATTLE OF NEW MARKET by William C. Davis,
Louisiana State University Press,
available at Amazon.com

VALLEY THUNDER by Charles R. Knight, Savas Beatie,
available at savasbeatie.com and Amazon.com

END OF AN ERA by John Sergeant Wise,
© University of North Carolina at Chapel Hill

Aerial Stock Video supplied by Skyworks and Image Bank Film/
Ghetty Images
Time Lapse Storm Video supplied by Thought Equity Motion and
RF Video+/Ghetty Images

VMI Aerial Footage supplied by Single Malt Media, LLC
Battle Stock Footage supplied by LionHeart FilmWorks, LLC

Arlington Confederate Monument photograph
supplied by Tim Evanson

Special Recognition

Commonwealth of Virginia
Virginia Fillm Office
Department of General Services
The Senate of VIrginia
The Virginia House of Delegates
The Virginia Executive Mansion
The Division of Capitol Police
Virginia Department of Corrections

Virginia Military Institute
General J.H. Binford Peay III, Superintendent
Pamela Peay, First Lady of VMI
Colonel Keith Gibson, Director VMI Museums
Colonel Stewart MacInnis, Director of Communications
Lieutenant Colonel Amy F. Goetz, Project Officer
VMI Public Works Department

New Market Battlefield State Historical Park
Virginia Museum of the Civil War
Major Troy D. Marshall, Director
Virginia Film Office

Andy Edmonds, Director
Historical Images Provided by
Virginia Military Institute Archives

Brandon L. Millett, Co-Founder and President,
G.I. Film Festival
Jason Netter

Special Thanks

Anne Farrell
Karen Kennedy
Brenda Long
Katherine Kennedy
Kenda Benward
Cadet Alyssa Ford
Dr. Ashleigh Kennedy, MD
Professor Craig Smith
Major General Sal Cambria, U.S. Army (retired)
Austin and Jane Brockenbrough
Peter and Christie Farrell
Stuart and Mary Farrell
Donald and Robbin Flow
Bill and Alice Goodwin
Bruce and Nancy Gottwald
Sam Kennedy
Charlie and True Luck
Tom and Sharon McNearney
Gil and Charlotte Minor
Bob and Sally Mooney
Rick Morgan
Bob and Louise Parsley
Jim and Bootsie Rogers
Tom and Scottie Slater

Bill and Kelley Stearman
Jim and Bobbie Ukrop
Don Wilkinson and Elaine Werner
Sam and Sally Witt

Andy Koyama
Charlize Toratani
Nancy Kirhoffer
Jes Vu
Jeff Striker

The Hotel Jefferson, Richmond, Virginia
Westover Plantation, Charles City County, Virginia
Candlewood Suites, Richmond, Virginia
Gettysburg Anniversary Committee and Rob Child

Notes

HISTORIAN'S NOTES – WILLIAM C. DAVIS

I came to the Battle of New Market by mistake as it happens. An old source said that my great-great-grandfather Josiah Davis's 45th Virginia Infantry regiment fought in the battle, and that made me curious to learn more about it. Later I found out that the old source was erroneous and the 45th Virginia was more than a hundred miles away at the time, a good object lesson in how fallible all history can be.

But the engagement still held my attention, and it is not hard to see why. It was a hair's breadth affair first to last. On paper the Federals should have overrun the Shenandoah, but they did not. Instead a former vice president of the United States commanding a scratch command rushed from all corners of southwest Virginia, managed to outwit and outfight the Yankees and save the vulnerable left flank of Robert E. Lee's army even then fighting for its life at Spotsylvania. And in the midst of it all were the corps of cadets from the Virginia Military Institute, rushed into the fighting line at a critical moment.

It was the stuff of myth and legend, and New Market, and

especially the role of the Cadets, has spawned a fair share of mythology over the years. As far back as the mid-1970s Frank McCarthy, the Oscar-winning producer of "Patton" and "MacArthur" dreamed of creating a film based on what might be called "the boys and the battle." Nothing came of that and other efforts, but now in "Field of Lost Shoes" we have at last a dramatic, realistic, and in the main accurate depiction of a great moment in the history of the Civil War, and for the VMI cadets the greatest moment of their lives.

Of course constraints of budget and clarity have forced the compression of time and some characters, but on the whole the creators of the film do little violence to the historical record, while opening the minds of a whole generation to the spirit as well as most of the facts of an epic event largely forgotten today except by students and historians. Moreover, they do so without glorifying war itself, or the Confederacy, or whitewashing the ugly underbelly of slavery. "Field of Lost Shoes" is in the tradition of generations of "coming of age" stories, only in the harshest and most dangerous of environments, the battlefield. It will resonate with all who have gone to war regardless of when or where, and remind those who have not of the terrible emotional and physical price all men and women in combat pay.

New Market remains a spirit in Virginia even today, especially in the Shenandoah Valley, and of course at the VMI. More than 7,000 men, Union and Confederate, seasoned soldiers and neophytes like the Cadets, struggled there in the rain and mud doing their small part in settling the greatest questions ever faced by Americans, including most of all just what sort of nation they were to be when the drums went still. Every generation confronts that question anew, and we should hope that they always will with the same courage and commitment of the men and Boys of New Market.

- William C. Davis, author, *The Battle of New Market*
(Louisiana State University Press, 1983)

HISTORIAN'S NOTES - CHARLES KNIGHT

The Battle of New Market is one of the great side stories of the Civil War. On paper it was a battle that the Confederates should have lost, but through a combination of skill, poor decisions on the other side, and a little old fashioned luck, a force of nearly all Virginia troops turned back a larger Union force.

The participants included a former Vice President of the United States (who also ran for president); the grandfather of one of the U.S. Army's greatest generals of World War II and the uncle of another; the son of Virginia's governor; the great nephew of the author of the Declaration of Independence; and a young man who would become one of the most famous sculptors of the nineteenth century.

The battle's fame far exceeds its size and scope. Did the Battle of New Market affect the outcome of the war? Absolutely not. But it did leave an indelible mark on those who participated, especially the cadets from Virginia Military Institute who found themselves taken from their classrooms and thrown into the chaos of battle, from which ten of their comrades would not return.

- Charles Knight, author, *Valley Thunder: The Battle of New Market* (Savas Beatie, 2010)

Recommended Reading

The Battle of New Market by William C. Davis
(Louisiana State University Press, 1983)

Valley Thunder: The Battle of New Market by Charles Knight
(Savas Beatie, 2010)

End of an Era by John S. Wise
(Available on line courtesy University of North Carolina)

Ghost Cadet by Elaine Marie Alphin
(Hither Page Press, 2010)

Recommended Listening

Field of Lost Shoes, Frederick Wiedman
(http://www.lalalandrecords.com/site/FOLS.html)

Made in the USA
Las Vegas, NV
20 March 2021